Piece of Clay

Alvin Riney

ISBN 978-1-63885-257-5 (Paperback)
ISBN 978-1-63885-258-2 (Digital)

Covenant Books, Inc.
11661 Hwy 707
Murrells Inlet, SC 29576
www.covenantbooks.com

INTRODUCTION

At the moment of conception, we are dependent on someone else to supply our every need. We have no choice. We are confined in a small cramped area for nine months. It is dark and damp. Sound filters in. Fluids are our nourishment. Some are bland. Some are spicy. Some are sweet. Some are sour. How we grow and develop is totally contingent upon the one who carries us and how they provide for us. We are at their mercy.

At birth, does much change?

We need someone to clothe, bathe, and feed us. We need someone to protect us. We come into this world void and shapeless. We are creatures of innocence. We see no color. We know no religion. We have no political affiliations. We are trusting. We are caring. We are loving. We are needy.

Our neediness is natural. How we grow, develop, and mature is contingent upon the ones who care for us. We are at their mercy.

Is it true our world shapes us? Do we really have any control over the influences around us? Do we have control over how those influences mold us?

"What you live is what you learn. What you learn is what you live." "The apple doesn't fall too far from the tree." "You are your father's child." "Like mother, like daughter."

We all have heard these sayings and more. How true are they? How binding are they? Because of where we come from and the lifestyle we grow up in, or because of who our parents are, does that predetermine our plight in life?

"What do you want to be when you grow up?"

That is a question that faces us all the moment we enter this world. It is what we see, hear, experience, and ultimately believe that helps us decide the answer to that question.

Our world fills us. It is what we do with what fills us that leads to our ultimate shape, our ultimate self. We are but a piece of clay.

Whom, or what, will we allow to be the potter?

Main Characters

Isabella (Bella) Seger—Seventeen-year-old faced with tragedy; trying to find her way in a new environment, plus facing an unimaginable horror.

Reahlin (Rey) McCullough—Seventeen-year-old superathlete with a secret.

Lametrius Brewer—High-powered wealthy defense attorney; driven to be the best and have the best.

Koen Brewer—Son of Lametrius Brewer and Kaneisha Edwards; professional counselor; has a somewhat shaky relationship with his father.

Tyler Davis—Midthirties adult who has had trouble staying out of trouble with the law for most of his life; doesn't seem like it's going to get better.

Hailey Crawford—Common-law wife of Tyler Davis; fragile esteem.

Brayden Davis—Son of Hailey Crawford and Tyler Davis; a teenager finding himself in a world of turmoil and trouble, trying to find a way out.

Deiondre Brown—Mayor of Elwood; a man of wealth, influence, and power.

Jamal Brown—Son of Mayor Deiondre Brown; superathlete with an ego problem.

Sgt. Jase Estes—Well-liked and revered officer with the Buchanan County Sheriff's Department.

Jaylyn Reese—Special assistant to Mayor Deiondre Brown; a socialite; romantic interest of Sgt. Jase Estes.

Prosecutor Jordan Luzier—Young prosecuting attorney with a great chess mind.

Lt. Marcus Riney—Member of the Buchanan County Drug Task Force; close friend of Sgt. Jase Estes.

Jolene Dooley—Fiancée and coworker of Koen Brewer.

Kaneisha Edwards—Ex-wife of Lametrius Brewer and mother of Koen Brewer.

Aunt Alicia—Aunt/guardian of Isabella (Bella) Seger.

CHAPTER 1

"So what do you think your father will think?" Kaneisha Edwards inquired.

"Why should I even worry about that? I am twenty-two years old. I believe I can decide for myself with something like this," answered her son, Koen Brewer.

"If that's the case, why did you come to me and ask me to give a vote of approval?"

"Mom, you know I've always come to you when I have big decisions to make. It's not that I'm always looking for approval. Sometimes I just need an objective insight."

"And a mother can give an objective opinion to her son, her only child, who just told her two minutes ago he is getting married to a girl his mother has never met? I don't know how objective I can be, quite honestly. I do think you can see my point."

"I would have to agree with you there," Koen conceded.

Kaneisha and Koen have not lived under the same roof for the last ten years. It was not a choice made by either one of them. Lametrius Brewer decided that for them.

Lametrius Brewer was a unique individual. His background would have led people to write him off as another victim of his environment. His father was doing prison time. The original conviction was for felonious assault and armed robbery. Prison did not serve as a place of rehabilitation for him. While serving his sentence for the assault and robbery, he was tried and convicted for his role in the death of two fellow inmates.

Lametrius's mother was never a mother. She spent the vast majority of her time entertaining male "friends." Her entertaining did help pay the bills, but it did not lend too much to quality time with her five children. She didn't cook. She didn't clean. She didn't discipline. She didn't love. How she ever escaped child services being called and her children taken away is a mystery.

Lametrius was the fourth of five children—two older sisters, an older and younger brother. With his siblings, the apple didn't fall too far from the tree. His older sisters had babies before they were sophomores in high school. His older brother lived the life of *Superfly* until the DEA swatted him. He went down in a blaze of gunfire.

Lametrius's younger brother, Chris, seemed to be on the right track. He loved school. He was active, athletic, and personable. He loved life. He was the type of child that people would get to know and say, "That child is going somewhere. That child is going to be somebody." Then one day, at the age of twelve, on Lametrius's fourteenth birthday, Chris didn't wake up. He was gone. The Lord decided it was time for him to come home. It was later discovered that he had a rare blood condition. A condition that was never treated because the family didn't have proper health coverage and health checkups.

The death was extra hard on Lametrius. You see, at that particular time, Lametrius was on that precarious fence in life—*which side do I want to be on? Which side do I belong on?* It would seem easy to surmise that he was probably leaning to the side of the fence his mother and older siblings were on. They would be the most likely *role models.* Yet such was not the case. Lametrius loved, admired, respected, and looked up to Chris. Chris was his role model. Chris's death changed Lametrius forever.

He knew how much people admired Chris. He wanted that to be him. He knew how people respected Chris. He wanted that to be him. He saw how people listened to Chris and saw how fluent and charismatic Chris was. He wanted that to be him. It wasn't that he was jealous or envious. He just wanted Chris to still be around. What better way to have that happen than to emulate him, to have Chris live through him.

Lametrius rededicated himself to school. He developed a strong drive and desire for success. He wanted nothing but the best. He worked toward nothing less than the best. He settled for nothing less than the best. He achieved nothing less than the best. He graduated as valedictorian of his high school class. He graduated magna cum laude from law school. He was hired by the second largest defense law firm in the state and, needless to say, given a healthy salary. He had worked his way up through the ranks and was able to establish his own lucrative practice. He was the best around.

Chris still lived in and through him. Chris still drove him. Yet somewhere along the way, Lametrius had gotten his priorities screwed up.

CHAPTER 2

Most high schools are a melting pot of races, cultures, ideas, identities, and values. The students try to navigate and figure out where they "belong," where they fit in, if at all.

Elwood High School was no different. The students were embroiled in a daily battle to be included, to feel relevant, needed, and wanted.

To some, school was an escape from home, a chance to get away and feel a sense of freedom. To others, school was like a prison, a place of physical and/or mental torture; a place filled with anxiety and dread. Still others loved being at school because they were a part of the in crowd, the cool kids. They felt an air of importance and validation, a sense of eliteness. For others, school was an extension of home; whatever was allowed or approved of at home was carried on to school.

"I'm not sure I can do that," stated Brayden Davis.

Mitchell didn't listen. "C'mon, man. It ain't gonna hurt nothin'. Just this once."

"Just this once?" Brayden replied. "This would be at least the tenth time. I can't afford to keep letting you slide. You've got to start taking care of business up front."

"Haven't I always come through and made things square with you?"

"No, you haven't. There's been many times I've had to come out of my pocket to make sure everything was right. I can't keep doing that. It's nothing personal. It's strictly from a business standpoint."

"I know, man. I know," relented Mitchell. "But I need something for the weekend. Help a brother out."

"I can't, man. Everything has to be accounted for today, and I don't have any spare change to cover you. Sorry, but no go."

"So you gonna do me like that? I see."

"I don't have a choice. Can't you understand my position?"

Mitchell probably did understand Brayden's position. But Mitchell didn't care about that. All Mitchell wanted was the next high, and he knew Brayden was the one who could fix him up. Ever since Brayden started junior high school, he had been conducting business for his father, Tyler Davis. He had learned the business well.

*****

Tyler Davis was on the road to being a gifted, spirited, and most likely successful individual. He had it all—charm, personality, good looks, and smarts. Everybody loved Tyler. He had a stable home. His mother and father provided a nice loving household. It was moderate, comfortable, clean, and full of love. The family wasn't rich, but the children didn't want for anything.

At the age of twelve, Tyler met a new kid named Frazier that had moved into the neighborhood. They became really good friends. When you saw one, you saw the other. Inseparable. One day, while the two were sitting in Frazier's bedroom, Frazier pulled a large wooden box from under his bed. When it was opened, Tyler's jaw dropped. He had never seen anything like it. There right in front of him was the largest accumulation of drugs he had ever seen outside of a pharmacy. There was an assortment of pills, all shapes, sizes, and colors. There were white and brown powders. There was a green leafy substance.

"Where did you get all this?" Tyler asked Frazier.

"I don't spend my allowance on just candy," Frazier replied.

That was when the experimenting began. Experimentation turned into casual use, which turned into addiction.

By age fourteen, Tyler was no longer the gifted, spirited, most likely successful person. His grades started failing. He became distant, paranoid, and suspicious of everyone. He had no true friends. Life in his household became a living hell. He was constantly in trouble with the law. He treated his parents with utter disrespect. He didn't follow house rules. He didn't pick up after himself. He stole from home. He let himself go physically. He didn't care about good hygiene. His parents began looking forward to the time they could kick him out of the house.

At sixteen, Tyler dropped out of school. He began spending more and more time away from home—days and weeks at a time. It got to the point that his parents stopped worrying about him and didn't attempt to find him when he was gone. In fact, life was happy and peaceful at the Davis household without him around.

Tyler met a young troubled teenage girl named Hailey Crawford when they were both being released from the county jail on the same day. They walked out together, talked a little, and discovered that neither one had a place they could go to and call home. From that day on, they have been together.

Within a year of their meeting, they parented a child. The responsibilities of parenthood did not change their lifestyle. The little baby boy was thrust into their dark world.

CHAPTER 3

"Yo, man! You were off the chain last season! They could do nothin' with you!" lauded Carlos Yeng.

Jamal Brown countered, "Man, it was like playing with babies. They couldn't handle this! I could've averaged fifty on 'em, but I had a little mercy. 'Cause that's the way I am."

"For real, dawg!" Carlos shouted.

"That was a real nice season, Jamal. You did a great job." Chimed in Jacob Eaton.

"Thanks, dawg. Hey, what's with the new girl?" asked Jamal. "How come nobody's introduced her to me yet?"

"Yeah, what's the deal?" Echoed Carlos.

"Carlos, shut up!" ordered Tiana King. Then she directed a question to Jamal. "Why don't you introduce yourself, Mr. Incredible?"

"I just might have to do that since the rest of you are slackin'," responded Jamal.

"Yeah, that's right!" Once again, echoed Carlos.

"Shut up, Carlos!" ordered Jacob and Tiana in unison.

The new girl they were referring to was Isabella, or Bella, Seger. She had been thrust into a new environment, the environment of Elwood, Kansas. She knew no one or nothing in or about the area—the school, the cliques, the city, nothing. But she was one who had always been able to adapt to whatever was thrown in front of her. Maybe that was because of her parents and how they had raised her.

Donna and Earl Seger had met in college. The saying says "opposites attract." Donna and Earl were the epitome of opposites. Donna was black. Earl was white. Donna was from the inner city north St. Louis, Missouri, and Earl was from the rural south, about fifteen miles south of Montgomery, Alabama. Donna was raised in a single-parent family, along with three siblings. Earl was raised in a solid family setting as an only child. Donna's family was of low-middle to low-socioeconomic status. Earl's family was of upper socioeconomic status and was very prominent socially and politically in the state. One would think these dramatic differences would create a barrier that: one, would not afford them an opportunity to meet, and two, would not be conducive to effective, productive dialogue. Yet it was just the opposite. Their differences sparked an interest that became so compelling, so infectious, so binding. Dialogue turned into friendship, friendship into affection, affection into love. The unlikeliest of unions became the hallmark of togetherness.

To this remarkable couple was born a beautiful baby girl named Isabella, who they called Bella. Donna and Earl made sure Bella was exposed to a variety of experiences, being careful not to overwhelm her. They taught her to be accepting to differences and not to be judgmental or prejudiced. Though the family was well off, they lived modestly. Donna and Earl did not want their daughter living a childhood of privilege because they feared what that might do to her in her adult life.

Bella loved her mother and father. She loved her life. She was such a well-adjusted child. She had a zest for life. She loved being around people. She loved the differences. She loved learning. Bella loved love. She could have been the poster child for the ideal daughter, friend, citizen, classmate, etc.

On Friday, June 19, Bella's seventeenth birthday, Donna and Earl were returning home from a trip to the local mall with presents for their almost-adult daughter. As they passed through a quiet intersection two blocks from home, they were broadsided by a speeding out-of-control Hummer. The impact was deafening. The collision was fatal. The death of Donna and Earl seemed to destroy the spirit of Bella.

Bella was shattered. Her world was turned upside down. The two people who had nurtured her, supported her in all her endeavors, taught her right and wrong, encouraged her independence and self-esteem, the two people who were supposed to be around to help her traverse the trials and tribulations of adulthood were suddenly gone. Never to return. Pure devastation.

Bella, battling through grief, was also faced with another dilemma now that her parents were gone—where was she to live?

There were no older siblings or grandparents that could take her in. There were, however, two aunts and one uncle on her mother's side of the family. But one aunt and the uncle were very reluctant and adamant they could not add a teenager to their already-challenging families. The other aunt was reluctant too. But her situation was different.

She was not married. She had no children. She was living a quiet private existence and did not want that disrupted. She balked, but eventually she was convinced that she was the only viable option to give Bella the opportunity to try to pick up the pieces and get a fresh start in an uncluttered environment.

So it was decided and worked out that Bella would move and live with her Aunt Alicia in Elwood, Kansas, a small city just across the state border from Drexel, Missouri.

CHAPTER 4

"Are you sure you don't want to talk for a little while?" Mr. King asked.

"Nah, man. I don't need to say nothing," Brayden answered.

Mr. King continued, "Sometimes it's best to get some things off your chest."

"Well, not today," Brayden said.

"I'm here to help."

"Man, how you gonna help? I'm already in trouble."

"Maybe if you open up a little, I might be able to—" Mr. King began.

"You can't do nothing!" interrupted Brayden. "You're just a counselor! All you want to do is hear all the details so you can get rid of me!"

"Brayden, your talks with me are confidential. I don't tell anybody about anything we discuss. You know that."

Brayden was not at all happy. He was sitting in the school counselor's office. He had moved there from the principal's office. Brayden had just gotten himself into a pretty big mess.

Brayden hasn't always been the best student, but he always managed to keep himself out of serious trouble. But today was different. It looked like he was definitely going to follow in his dad's footsteps. He had finally been caught running afoul of the law.

It was like any other day. The routine was the same. Nothing appeared out of place—the location, the time, the clientele. Maybe that was the problem. Maybe everything had gotten too routine. Maybe he had become too sure of himself.

How could this happen? What was Dad going to say? Out of all the concerns facing him at that moment, that last question was the most daunting. It wasn't that he feared disappointing his dad. That was not the issue. He was concerned about the for-certain beating he was going to get at the hands of his dad. Dad was about to lose out on one of his biggest money-making venues. Dad didn't like losing money.

Mr. King received a phone call. "Okay. Send them on down." He hung up.

"The police are here, Brayden. If you ever feel the need to talk to someone, I'm always available. Any time. Day or night. I'm serious."

Brayden just nodded. Dread began to creep over him. It wasn't like he hadn't seen the police come around and haul someone away. Usually it had been his mom or dad. It was different now because he was the one being carted off. *Where am I going? How are they going to treat me? How long will I have to be there? Is it clean or dirty? What am I going to do?* As questions kept bombarding his mind, the uniformed police officers entered the room.

"How are you doing?" Officer Tyes greeted Mr. King.

"I'm fine, thank you. Officers, this is Brayden."

Mr. King gestured toward Brayden, who sat leaning forward, head down, looking at the floor.

"Brayden, stand up, turn around, put your hands behind your back," ordered Officer Walton. "You are under arrest for possession with the intent to distribute. You have the right to remain silent…"

It was not a dream. It was harsh reality. Brayden knew it could happen, but up until then, he believed it never would happen. He thought to himself, *Here I go. I'm just like Dad. I hope he's satisfied. This is not what I wanted. Why did I let this happen? What's going to be in store for me now?*

His thoughts were interrupted by Officer Walton.

"Do you understand these rights as I have read them to you?"

"Yeah," Brayden answered.

"Understanding these rights, do you wish to make any statements at this time?" continued Officer Walton.

"No," responded Brayden.

"It's time to go," said Officer Tyes.

As Brayden was being led out of the office, Mr. King stated, "Brayden, don't forget. I'm always available. Really."

Brayden did not respond as the trio left the office and headed for what would be Brayden's resting place for the next several hours.

CHAPTER 5

It had been several months since the tragic accident that had killed Bella's parents, but the pain was still evident and very real. Plus it didn't make things any easier by having to adapt to completely new surroundings. Bella was in a new city. She knew no one. She was at a new school and knew no one.

It seems especially tough to get to know others when you are a senior. It seems like everyone else has known each other for years, and their cliques have already been established. It appears impossible for an outsider to be accepted into any particular group.

High school can be tough. Not only the academics but especially the social scene. Bella realized that and had told herself to concentrate on her classes. She knew she had to make the grades if she was going to be able to go to college and study forensics. So that was what she did. She was an excellent student.

After another normal lonely day at school, Bella was passing through the commons area on her way home.

"Hey! Bella's your name, right?"

"Umm, yeah," Bella responded.

"I thought so. I'm Reahlin. Everybody calls me Rey or Rey J. Pleased to meet you."

"Good to meet you too."

"Have you gotten a chance to meet a lot of people?" Rey inquired.

"Not really. You're actually the first one I've really had a chance to say more than hi to. Everything seems so hectic."

"Don't sweat it. It'll all slow down. Hey, do you play any sports? 'Cause if you do, I might be able to fill you in on what's what."

"Well, I played a little basketball. I was okay. I could play some defense, but I couldn't shoot that well. I haven't played for about a year," Bella offered.

"Don't worry 'bout that. We need somebody that knows how to D-up. Tryouts begin in a few days. You oughta think about trying out. I play and maybe could help you along. What do you think?" Rey continued.

"I don't know. I'll talk it over with my aunt and let you know."

"Great! I gotta go. See you tomorrow. Don't forget. Think about it," commented Rey as she was leaving.

Bella felt kind of good inside. She had been at the new school for a couple months, and this was the first actual conversation she had had. What Bella didn't know was that she had just been conversing with the number 1 rated female basketball player in the state. Rey seemed very nice. She reminded Bella of her best friend back in Hill City, Kansas; a friend she had lost touch with since the tragedy.

Bella's Aunt Alicia had her own theory of how Bella should deal with the horrible situation. Aunt Alicia's idea was to remove Bella completely away from everything she knew that was related to her life with her parents. She moved her away from her hometown, her school, her friends. She cut her off from any communication with her closest friends—no calling, no social media, nothing. Bella thought all this was completely wrong, but what could she do? Aunt Alicia was the only family willing and capable of taking her in. Bella was sharp enough and raised properly enough to realize that rebellion would not be a smart move.

CHAPTER 6

Several days later, Koen was discussing with his father, Lametrius Brewer, what he had previously discussed with his mother.

"What!" shouted Brewer as he was seated in his den, talking to his son, Koen.

"I'm ready," answered Koen.

"What do you mean ready? How can you say you're ready?" Brewer continued to question.

"I've got a steady job. She works. We're looking at getting a nice place."

Lametrius refused to see anything good in Koen's decision.

"You've got a job, but it can't support a family. Counseling doesn't pay much, and you're at the bottom now."

"There's only one way to go, and that's up," quipped Koen.

"Right! In today's economy, institutions like you work for are cutting services left and right. You'd be the first to go."

"I'm not concerned about that. If it happens, it happens. I love Jolene."

"Love won't pay your bills! So Jolene is her name. Jolene who? I might have run across some of her family."

"I doubt it, Dad. Jolene Dooley. She recently relocated into the area. Her family is from around Memphis."

"How old? What kind of job?"

"She's thirty-two. Works at the same counseling service I do."

"Thirty-two!"

"Before you ask, yes, she's been married once before. No children."

"Son, I thought I raised you to be smarter. Can you not see the writing on the wall? This is a disaster just waiting to happen."

"How you figure?" Koen was starting to get perturbed.

"Listen, son. Thirty-two. Working as a counselor. After relocating. Probably running from something or someone. Probably still on the infamous rebound. Latching on to a not-so-experienced not-so-logical kid ten years her junior—"

"Whoa! Whoa! Whoa!" interrupted Koen. "Who you calling not so logical?"

"I think it's quite obvious who I am talking about. How long have you known her?"

"About four months."

"How long has she been in the counseling field?"

"About four months."

Brewer continued his seemingly relentless questioning. "What did she do before that?"

"She was a pharmacist."

"What! How long did she do that?"

"About seven years."

"Evidently she's not very logical either," criticized Brewer. "How can a person in their right mind give up a career that took a lot of hard work to get into and will maintain its status of necessity for a long time and pays six figures automatically? Who throws that away?"

"She didn't throw it away. She walked away. It wasn't what she wanted. It didn't fulfill her need to help others. Her husband thought like you, and he left her."

"Smart man," quipped Brewer. "Son, how do you know she won't do the same to you—find out down the road that you don't fulfill her? Will she walk away from you?"

"Do I know 100 percent for sure that she won't change her mind? No, I don't. But I don't believe she would do that to me. We have a genuine connection, a special kind of connection. No one really thinks the worst when they meet that special someone. Did you when you met Mom?"

"Actually I looked at it as a business venture, and she appeared to be a suitable business partner. As you see, it didn't work out."

"What! How cold hearted are you? Have you ever really loved beyond your expensive toys? I sincerely doubt it! I hope to God I am never like you! You'll get an invitation. Show up if you want. Either way, no big deal!" Koen exited angrily and hurriedly.

CHAPTER 7

"I don't believe it! I just don't believe it!"

Tyler Davis was beside himself with a myriad of emotions—anger, paranoia, fear, disappointment. How could his son do this to him? He wondered if Brayden knew what the consequences could be for his father, how long he could be locked up. Tyler was paranoid and afraid. He didn't know whether he should go to the police department and pick up his son or just leave him there. He had no idea if Brayden had told them everything or not. Tyler knew that his son was not as hardened as he was at seventeen years of age. He knew that Brayden was not as familiar with police tactics as he was. Tyler's fear and paranoia outweighed his anger and disappointment, for the moment.

Tyler stated, "I don't think we should go to the station."

"What! You're kidding, right?" asked Hailey incredulously.

"I'm serious!" responded Tyler. "It's probably some setup to get us down to the station and arrest us. I don't trust them! I just know they got Brayden to tell them everything about everybody."

Hailey couldn't believe what she was hearing. "Still, I can't leave my baby down there."

"We can't go down there!!"

"We have to!" Hailey insisted. "They said they needed us both to come down."

"Don't you find that a little strange? They need both of us? That's a setup if I've ever seen one!"

"We're going, whether we get arrested or not!" demanded Hailey.

Tyler was now angered. "That's what you think, do you? Woman, you don't tell me what we're going to do! You never have, and you ain't gonna start now!"

"Tyler, please. We have to go. Please?"

"Woman, nothin' good is gonna come out of this! Nothing, I tell you! Where's my keys? Is everything locked up? I'm not ready to be locked down again! Let's go! Man, why wasn't he more careful? What was he thinking? How could he do this to me? I don't believe it! I just don't believe it!"

The two of them departed from their home, headed for what might possibly be an extended stay in a secure county facility.

CHAPTER 8

Bella took Rey up on the invitation to try out for the basketball team. The only comforting sight in the gym was Rey. Everyone else looked familiar. They were the same ones who passed her every day in the halls at school. The same ones who never spoke but always made it a point to give her a you're-not-welcome-here kind of look. The same looks she was getting right now. Even Rey didn't come up to speak to her. Rey just kind of kept off to the side, almost by herself.

Coach Mac entered the gymnasium. All the girls stopped their idle chatter. Coach Mac, at first appearance, was an intimidating-looking man. He stood about 6'4", lean, well built. He had a walk that said *I mean business, and don't give me any business.*

"Good afternoon, ladies," bellowed Coach Mac.

The thirty-two girls present responded in unison, "Hi, Coach!"

"I'm so pleased to see so many of you ladies out here today. As you know, today is day one of three days of tryouts for the girls' basketball team. Varsity only is right now! If you are here for any other squad, JV or freshman, that is later this evening."

Four girls left immediately, looking rather embarrassed.

"Looks like I have about twenty-five or so girls trying out, but I only have twelve spots. If you think the odds are too long, you may leave now." No one left. "That's what I like to see. No quitters, no matter what the odds. Some of you played last year. I want you to realize that does not guarantee you a spot this year. As always, you've got to earn what you get."

Looks of trepidation began to move across the faces of about half the girls. Looks of doubt was evident on one-fourth. The others remained stoic. Bella was one of them. She also had the strange feeling that she was being closely scrutinized by Rey. If it were true, she had no idea why.

Coach Mac continued, "I could stand here and talk to you all day, but it's time to get moving. One more thing, though. This is very important. When I blow this whistle, everything stops—the basketballs, your mouths, the air flow, everything. And if I'm explaining anything to anybody, I want your undivided attention. I get very upset when somebody's talking when I'm talking. When I'm perturbed, consequences will be forthcoming. Discipline is important to success, so you might as well get started with the notion right off the bat. All right. 'Nough said. Give me ten laps in three minutes. Go!"

So the fun began.

Bella, Rey, and about four other girls seemed to love the grueling three days of tryouts. Every drill and challenge were met with 100-percent commitment. A few girls did not return for day 2 of tryouts, and the same was the case for day 3. Nineteen girls were left to fill twelve spots. Bella was hopeful yet not overly confident. It felt good to be involved in a team activity again. One thing puzzled her, though.

Ever since the conversation in the commons, Rey hadn't spoken to Bella, even at tryouts. It appeared as if she was trying to avoid Bella. During certain drills, it seemed like Rey was more aggressive toward her than the other girls. Bella played it off and kept moving. Just when she thought a breakthrough had come and her social life might improve, she realized she was still out there, all alone.

In a little more than eighteen hours, Bella would know if her efforts were good enough to impress Coach Mac and earn a spot on the team. All she could do now was wait.

CHAPTER 9

Koen continued to seethe once he got home to his fiancée, Jolene.

"I don't want you upset with your father," said Jolene.

"Too late," said Koen.

"He's just trying to look out for your best interest."

"What, he doesn't think I'm capable of doing that on my own?"

"Are you?" teased Jolene.

Koen, smiling, replied, "Yes, I am, Ms. Lady."

"Well, what do you have to worry about then?"

"It's just so aggravating! He always thinks he's right. He always thinks he has the answers. He can judge but can't be judged. When he said he only looked at Mom as a business partner, that was it! I don't ever want to be like him. He is selfish, egotistical, narcissistic, and rude. In other words, he's an ass!"

"He's your father, Koen. He loves you. I know you know that. He just has peculiar ways of showing it."

"Everything has to be his way. Nobody does anything as well as he does. No one is as good as he is at anything. All I can remember, ever since I was a little kid, he has tried to mold me and shape me. Not into what I wanted to be. It was what he wanted me to be. What he thought I should do to be successful. He wanted me to be him. My decisions were his decisions. His decisions were my decisions. He is so driven to have the best of everything."

"Well, don't you want the best?"

"Yes, I do. But I want the best of the important nonmaterial things. All he cares about is image, flashiness. I can't travel that road."

Jolene asked, "Having been raised with him being your primary caregiver, how did you get to be so well rounded?"

"My mother. For some reason, he always tried to drive a wedge between me and Mom. But the harder he tried, the closer we got. Mom is a remarkable woman. You're going to love her. She's anxious to meet you. I've said some pretty nice things about you. Don't make me out to be a liar."

"You'll just have to wait and see now, won't you?" countered Jolene.

CHAPTER 10

The girls all gathered around, trying to get a good look at the list. Bella, not being too well liked, so it seemed, hung back until most of the girls cleared out. There were shrieks of joy, high fives, tears of disappointment, shrugs of indifference, angry utterances. Bella was growing more and more nervous. She stepped closer. For some reason, she really wanted to see her name up there. It was almost like she needed to see her name on that list. She had never had such a yearning before. She didn't quite understand why.

As she got close enough to see clearly, she shut her eyes, exhaled deeply, and then looked. Her heart sank. Sadness and disappointment swept over her entire being. Her name was not on the list. She just stood there for what seemed like a short eternity, just staring at the list. She finally managed to turn away from the board and began walking toward the commons. She was about halfway across the commons when she thought she heard her name faintly called. Without turning to look around, she kept walking toward the exit.

"Hey, Bella!"

This time, there was no mistake. Somebody had called her name. She turned to see Rey hurrying across the commons, waving both arms. Bella reluctantly stopped.

"Hey, how you doing?" asked Rey.

"Okay," quietly said a noticeably saddened Bella.

"Well, you look and sound a little down."

"Guess I'm just a little tired," offered Bella.

"I saw you coming from over there, looking at the list. Didn't see your name?"

Bella just nodded.

"You're looking like you need a pick-me-up," Rey commented.

"I don't think anything could pick me up right now. I wanted to make the team so badly. I was so excited. I thought I did okay. I don't know. I just need to go home and gather myself."

Rey said, "I don't think you really need to do that."

"What? Why wouldn't I?"

"When you looked at the list," began Rey, "how many names were on there?"

Bella was confused now. "What? Twelve!"

"Are you sure?"

"Yeah, I'm sure," said Bella. "Well, I didn't actually count them."

"Maybe you should have. There's only eleven names on that list."

"What? Why would there be just eleven? Coach Mac said there would be twelve spots."

"That's correct," affirmed Rey.

"Well, I don't get it. Are they going to fill the twelfth spot or not?"

"They already have," Rey informed Bella.

Bella was totally confused at that point. "You've got me lost! Why are you talking in riddles?"

Rey decided to clear things up for Bella.

"Okay, just listen for a minute. You don't know yet, but I've earned some special privileges as a member of this team. You see, I've been playing basketball for Coach Mac for what seems like forever—YMCA, summer leagues, you name it. He's not only my coach, he's my adoptive father. So I've got the inside scoop on a lot of the things that go on with the team. I kind of peeked at the list, saw the names, and asked for a special favor."

"Really? So you know who the twelfth player is?"

"That's right." Beamed Rey. "When I saw the list, I asked him to list just eleven and let me be the one to tell the twelfth girl. At first he refused, but after some serious begging, he gave in."

"Why?"

"Why what?"

"Why would you want to be the one to tell the last person?"

Rey was visibly excited.

"Well, I just thought it might be pretty cool to see how excited you'd be to get the good news, one-on-one!"

"You...What...Are...Am...Did..."

"You got it! You made the team!" confirmed Rey.

"Are you sure? This is not just some cruel joke on the new girl, is it?"

"Nope. This is real. You are officially an Elwood Lady Bulldog!"

Bella was extremely ecstatic. Wow! How emotions can swing in a matter of minutes, seconds for that matter. This is the happiest she has been since moving to Elwood.

Bella had to ask, "But why did you want to be the one to tell me? I haven't talked to you for more than a week. I figured you decided to be like everybody else and shun me. And at tryouts! Why were you so rough on me? I just knew right then you didn't like me."

Rey explained, "I've always liked you from our first conversation. When I thought that there might be a chance that you would try out for the basketball team, I figured it would be best to keep my distance and be a little standoffish."

"But why?"

"You sure ask a lot of whys!" Observed Rey. "Anyway I figured if you were any good, you could prove it on your own, and nobody would think you made it only because you were friends with the coach's daughter. Plus I wanted to see what you had myself. I didn't even tell Coach I knew you."

An elated and appreciative Bella said, "Thanks. That means a lot."

Rey continued, "Hey, now that we're teammates, maybe we can exchange numbers, call or text each other and hang out some."

"You bet," agreed Bella. "Let me get some paper."

Were things finally turning around for Bella? It certainly seemed like it. This was the happiest she'd been since right before the news of the tragedy.

CHAPTER 11

Elwood is your basic twenty-first-century small yet steadily growing city. It has two US highways running through the middle of it and an interstate highway running along its western edge. It is about thirty miles northwest of the nearest major metropolis. Yet it has just about everything a person would want, readily available in its up-to-date businesses. It boasts of having many of the regionally favorite restaurant chains, grocery stores, department stores, fast-food restaurants, entertainment venues, etc. Everything a person could want, plus all the drama.

Elwood's history parallels that of most other small towns in America. It started out as a quaint little community where everybody knew everybody. Neighbor talked to neighbor. People were more than willing to step up and help a neighbor in need, not looking for anything in return; a true community.

As the town grew into a city, a gap began to develop among the residents. The bigger the city grew, the wider the gap became. People were so busy within their own little worlds they didn't take the time to get to know their neighbor. They barely spoke to one another.

As all across this country, there developed a schism between the youth and adults of Elwood. The youth showed no respect nor paid any homage to their elders. The attitudes of the community were magnified in the school community at the high school.

Over the past three years, hard work, commitment, respect for authority, pride in one's self, school pride, dedication, reliability—all these things seemed to be in short supply at the home of the Bulldogs. Yes, there were those few athletes who stayed in the gym or the weight room, trying to get better, trying to gain an advantage. They were few and far between. There were the members of the different clubs, National Honor Society, Drama Club, FCA, FBLA, etc., all whose numbers were in steady decline. At the same time, the dropout rate was on the rise, as was the enrollment at the alternative school. ISS (in-school suspension) was always full. Classroom behavior was atrocious. Students barely listened to the instructors' lectures. They would rather text or sleep. Teachers got to the point that they ignored the distractions rather than write the perpetrators up because the administration was so overwhelmed with discipline issues. They had to order a moratorium on referrals to the office. This year promised to be different.

Dr. Earlis T. Cooke was hired as principal to bring about a change to this eroding environment. A product of a tough inner-city upbringing, Dr. Cooke had the courage, strength, experience, and stick-to-itness to see the task through to completion. Dr. Cooke knew that changes were necessary, not only with the students but with the faculty and staff as well. Low morale and apathy ran rampant through the staff.

Dr. Cooke moved a lot of teachers around. The weak teachers were not rehired or put in positions requiring less skill. The know-it-alls were placed in unfamiliar, more challenging roles. The strong, dedicated, student-centered teachers were put in grade-leader positions. It was made perfectly clear that backbiting, backstabbing, bad-mouthing, negative attitudes toward peers and coworkers would not be tolerated at all. Such behavior would result in a job target or even dismissal. Dr. Cooke was a firm believer in the philosophy that cohesiveness at the top lends to a smooth-running workplace. Because how can you manage students if you can't manage yourselves? How can you effectively educate students if your attention is diverted by negative thoughts or actions directed toward a coworker or if you are the target of such negative behaviors?

The students were also starting to get the message that Dr. Cooke did not play. With the culture having sunk so low, it was going to take some time to get everybody in step. Though the school year was young, progress was being made.

Because of Dr. Cooke's no-nonsense no-tolerance policies, the chance that Brayden would be back to complete coursework, earn the required credits, and walk with his classmates was pretty slim. One might say his chances were slim to none.

CHAPTER 12

The Elwood Bulldogs have been an up-and-coming girls' basketball team the last few seasons. But what else would you expect having a player the caliber of Rey? They just couldn't get past sectionals the last two years because of the Connelly Warriors.

The first ten games of this new season gave the Bulldog fans reason to believe things would be different this year. Rey was playing like she was definitely on a mission. She was already the best around, but it seemed as though she had gotten much better. There was no stopping her. Opposing coaches could only sit back, shake their heads, and watch the show. What made matters worse for the opposition was that it looked like Elwood had found that missing piece of the puzzle needed to get them over the top. That missing piece was Bella Seger.

"Yo, Jamal, the Bulldog girls are hoopin'!" Carlos said.

"So I hear," responded Jamal.

"You haven't watched them play yet?" Jacob asked.

"Man, you know I don't watch no girls play! That's whack!" bragged Jamal.

"But, man, they be killin'!" shouted Carlos.

"And your point?" Jamal questioned.

"I hear you haven't even had a conversation with that Bella girl." Jacob pointed out.

Jamal stated, "In due time. I don't need to rush."

"It might be easier to get a conversation if she saw you at one of her games," suggested Tiana. "That's just coming from a female's point of view."

"Y'all ain't getting ready to go all Dr. Phil on me, are you? 'Cause I ain't listenin'!" Jamal said.

"That's your problem, Jamal. You never listen. You think you know it all and can do it all..." added Tiana.

"Hey, hey! Don't be jumpin' all over me. I am who I am. I can't help that it's all good."

"Yeah, ain't his fault it's all good." Echoed Carlos.

"Shut up, Carlos!" shouted Tiana and Jacob in unison.

Jamal was a one-of-a-kind special athlete. Yet he lacked several endearing qualities.

At an early age, it was evident he was athletically gifted. He excelled at everything he tried. He could run. He could throw. He could jump. He could swim. If there was the opportunity to try gymnastics and/or ballet, it was probably a sure bet he would be the best around. His abilities so outshone his age group that he had to participate against older children to get any sort of real competition. He was used to hearing and having praises heaped upon him. He grew to expect it. It got to the point that if others didn't exhort the accolades, he would do it himself. You see, the constant pouring of praise and accolades turned him into an arrogant, egotistical sort of person.

Jamal did, to his credit, work extremely hard on his skills. He took great care of his body, e.g., eating the right foods, carefully sculpting his body, always in the gym, etc. He was a good-looking handsome young man. Everybody knew it. Worst of all, he knew it. Few people wanted to hang out with him. Those that did were the needy—i.e., needy in the sense they had no identity of their own. They needed validation for their existence.

CHAPTER 13

"Come in. Have a seat." Directed Dr. Cooke.

Brayden and his mother, Hailey, entered the principal's office. Brayden didn't want to be there. He knew what was about to happen, what he was about to hear. Plus he was worried if there was still noticeable swelling and bruising. If so, that would most assuredly lead to inquiry; an inquisition he wanted no part of because he didn't want to tell the story. He didn't want to talk about the pain, the fear, the anger, the disgust he had experienced. He already relived it over and over in his mind, day after day, night after night.

Eight Days Ago

"What the hell were you thinking!" A slap to the face of Brayden. "You're about the dumbest son of a bitch on the face of the earth!" A hard kick to the shin. "I can barely stand to look at you!" Punch to the face. "What did you tell them?" Another punch to the face. "What did you tell them?" A kick to the groin. "Answer me, boy! Answer me!"

Barely able to catch his breath, Brayden weakly responded, "Nothing. I didn't say nothing."

Brayden knew during the ride home from the police station what was in store. He knew his dad was angry, furious. But he never envisioned such a pounding. He had never seen his dad so out of control. For one whole hour, nothing but misery and abuse.

"Do you realize what you've done? What were you thinking? What are we going to do now?" Tyler continued to rant.

The one-way conversation went on and on. It seemed like it would never end. But Brayden figured he would have a lot of time to heal due to his long-term suspension.

*****

Dr. Cooke extended his right hand. Hailey, then Brayden, shook his hand, trying not to look him directly in the eyes.

"Brayden, this is the first time I've had an opportunity to meet you."

Dr. Cooke continued, "You've been out of school for quite some time. As you know, being out of school means you fall behind, and the grades drop. Because of your long-term suspension, the district policy does not allow you the chance to get the work you're missing out on. Having said such, why do you think I had you come in today?"

Shrugging his shoulders, Brayden responded softly, "I don't know."

"No idea at all?"

"Well, I kinda figured that because of what I did, I'm here to get the official determination from the school," Brayden guessed.

"And what do you think that would be?"

Brayden thought for a few seconds, then quietly, reluctantly, said, "Expulsion."

"Excuse me? I didn't quite hear you," Dr. Cooke said.

"Expulsion."

Dr. Cooke smiled, nodded his head. "As I looked over your records, you've never been in any serious trouble. You make decent grades, and I'm sure if you really applied yourself, the grades would be even better. Your attendance is great. Does all that sound right?"

Brayden gave a quiet nod.

Dr. Cooke moved on. "Have either of you ever heard of S-M-A-R-T, SMART?"

Brayden and Hailey shook their heads no.

"Well, it stands for socially maladjusted at-risk teens, SMART. It's a program that the district is just starting up. It's an alternative school of sorts. The district and the courts are working cooperatively in an effort to give some of our youth a second chance."

Brayden became more interested but continued to sit silently.

"There are three components to the program, academics, court-ordered probation, and counseling. The court puts you on probation for whatever offense you may have committed. As a condition of your probation, you'll be required to attend arranged classes on a regular basis, around 90-percent attendance per a quarterly graded period. You must maintain a minimum of a *C* average and receive no discipline write-ups. Also there will be court-ordered counseling—group and individual. It will be one two-hour session per week. As you might realize, any misstep would mean a revocation of your probation, and since you are seventeen, it's no more juvenile. It's playing with the big boys now." Dr. Cooke paused for a few seconds, then asked, "How do you think SMART sounds? Are you interested?"

CHAPTER 14

Rey said to Bella, "Well, well. Look who showed up at a girls' basketball game. Mr. Stud himself. Wonder what got him here?"

Bella, after a warm-up shot, looked in the direction Rey was indicating and saw Jamal and his entourage.

Rey continued, "I guess you know he thinks girls' basketball is nothing. To him it is too slow and boring."

"Well, I guess we need to show him what it's really all about," commented Bella.

They high-fived each other and continued with their spirited pregame drills.

What took place on the court during the course of the game could only be described as simply artistic.

The Bulldogs' opponent was their nemesis, the Connelly Warriors, the same team that had knocked them out of the post season the last two seasons. The game was close for about thirty seconds. The Warriors were completely dismantled by the Bulldogs. At halftime, the score was 48–19. The second half was even more brutal on the Warriors. They looked nothing like a state semifinal team, and the Bulldogs looked like world champions. It was beautiful, simply beautiful.

Final score: 99–31.

Rey had a game-high, twenty-seven points to go along with eleven rebounds, five steals, and five assists in one and a half quarters. Bella pitched in with sixteen points, ten boards, eight steals, and fifteen assists in two quarters. The media had played this game up to be the game of the year. It wasn't even close. However, it was a statement game, and the basketball world got the message—loud and clear. This was the year of the Bulldog!

"Good game, ladies," Jamal complimented.

"Thanks," accepted Rey. "Well, what got you to walk in the gym and stay to watch a girls' basketball game? You did watch, didn't you? Or were you too busy signing autographs?"

"Now, now. All that ain't necessary. I did watch, and I was quite impressed. You girls are not too bad."

"Not too bad!" Rey turned to walk away. "C'mon, Bella. Let's go."

Bella turned to follow.

"Excuse me. But I don't think we've been formally introduced."

Bella stopped and turned to face Jamal. He extended his hand.

"I'm Jamal. I've seen you around but haven't had the opportunity to make your acquaintance."

She accepted his hand. "I'm Bella. Nice to meet you."

Rey just shook her head and moved on to the locker room.

*****

Bella and Jamal seemed to hit it off quite nicely. Jamal attended more and more *girls'* basketball games and seemed to really get into them. Bella went to watch Jamal and the boys' varsity play. She saw that Jamal was truly the real deal. They spent a lot of time together.

"Where you guys going this weekend?" inquired Rey.

"Nowhere that I know of. Probably just watch a movie or play video games at his house," answered Bella.

"I've told you before, be careful. He…" Rey hesitated. "I don't know. Just be careful."

"Is there something I should know?" Bella asked.

"There's nothing that I know. I just want you to be careful and not get hurt."

"I'm being careful, taking things slow," assured Bella. "Jamal's been nothing but nice to me. I know he has his attitudes, but he's good people. I really like him."

"Just be careful," Rey warned.

Rey had only heard things. She wasn't one to say something unless she knew it to be fact. The rumor mill was not her cup of tea.

Bella, meanwhile, was on cloud nine. Her life was at an all-time high. Her best friend was the best; MVP, all-state, all-conference, a great confidante—you name it. The love of her life was no slouch either; handsome, MVP, all-state, all-conference, self-assured—you name it. And she was making a name for herself, a positive mark. Things couldn't be better.

CHAPTER 15

Koen and Jolene were the architects of the SMART (socially maladjusted at-risk teens) program. They were preparing for the very first session.

"I think this is a great idea," Jolene encouraged Koen.

"Yeah, but the pressure is on," said Koen. "After all the lobbying and politicking we had to do, we had better be sure we make it work. This is the pilot program."

"Why wouldn't it work? Two young energetic people in charge. Backing of the courts and school…"

"Yeah, but you realize the clientele, right? If they don't want it, it will not work."

"We'll make them want it. It'll be so good, they'll be begging for more," Jolene said.

"I sure hope you're right." Koen had his doubts.

The meeting room was located in a conference room on the second floor of the US Bank building. At around 4:35 p.m., the clientele began arriving. By 4:55 p.m., everyone who had been signed up had signed in; twelve in all.

Koen and Jolene introduced themselves, told a little about their lives, and discussed the program—the who, what, why, how.

The first session was a meet and greet. All the clientele gave their name, a rundown on how they got there, and what they hoped to get out of SMART.

"Yo, I'm DaRon. Don't really know why I'm here. I was told to show up, so here I am. Two hours is what you get."

"My name's Tami. Supposedly I was soliciting. Now do I look like I'd be doin' something like that? For real! So here I am. Personally I think it's a bunch of bull."

That's how it went; one after another, until Brayden spoke.

"Hey, my name is Brayden. I'm seventeen. I'm not really one to talk about my personal business, but seeing as part of my probation is taking part in this program, I'm planning on doing what I need to do to clear my name and prove I'm not all bad. I'm here for selling drugs at school. I hope this SMART program will show me a different road to take. I've known only one road, and I've always known it was wrong, but you gotta do what you can to get by."

As Brayden spoke, Koen could sense the sincerity in his voice. It gave Koen a lift. He knew that if there was at least one who was going to be there for all the right reasons, the program was going to start off on the right foot.

It seemed like the last three to talk picked up their cue from Brayden. They knew why they were there and what positive things they wanted to get from the program.

Koen and Jolene were beaming. They already knew they had put together an awesome program, and all they needed to make it work was willing and able clientele. Now they had just that—four or five who really wanted to better their situation and, more importantly, better themselves.

The last hour of the first session was a social hour. Everybody mingled, ate snacks, and engaged in small talk. Right at seven o'clock, Koen and Jolene dismissed the group.

As Brayden reached the sidewalk in front of the building, DaRon approached him.

"Yo, so you can cop some dope?" DaRon wanted to know.

"What?" Brayden was taken aback by the question and DaRon's brashness.

"So you said you could get some stuff?"

"I never said that," Brayden denied.

"But you could, right?" DaRon was unrelenting.

"No!" Brayden snapped back.

"You said you was selling."

"I said I was. I don't do that anymore," Brayden confirmed.

"So you say. If the money was right, I'd bet you'd get right back into the game," argued DaRon. "Tell you what, I'll get back to you next week with some figures and see if that don't change your mind."

Brayden asserted, "You'll be wasting your time and breath."

"We'll see. Talk to ya later."

As DaRon walked away, Brayden just shook his head. He realized more and more each day how difficult it was going to be to live down the reputation and negative stigma he had attached to himself. His own dad was making preparations to get him back in the game. That was one of the many reasons Brayden hated to be at home. That's all his dad would talk to him about, as if there was nothing more important. Granted, the household did suffer a loss of a big chunk of income, illegitimate though it may have been. Brayden could only think that if his mom and dad would get off their lazy butts, they could make some decent money. But that would be too much like right.

He began his slow lonely trek back home.

Home was not a place Brayden wanted to be anymore. There was nothing there but pain, misery, and abuse. He didn't know how much more he could take, yet he had no idea what he could do.

Who would've thought life could, or would, be so difficult at seventeen years of age?

CHAPTER 16

The Lady Bulldogs were a huge draw throughout the season, at home and on the road. Every venue was standing-room only. Their average margin of victory was just over fourteen points per game. Their off nights were as good as any other team's best night. It just so happened that tonight was the worst of the worst games.

They were playing the Janson Flyers for what would decide the conference title and have an impact on the district seedings. A win by the Bulldogs, and number 1 was all theirs—conference and the district seeding.

The Bulldogs seemed to have a missing cylinder. They never got any type of flow going throughout the game. As the game wore on, the Flyers gained more and more confidence. With forty-five seconds to go in the game, the Flyers led by two. It was their ball to inbound. The Bulldogs allowed the inbound. They then applied the clamps.

What hadn't been evident all game suddenly sprang into being. A steal and a layup. Full-court press. A steal and a layup. Full-court press. A steal and a jumper. Just like that, with twenty-seconds seconds remaining, the Bulldogs were up by four. Token full-court pressure caused another turnover. The Bulldogs simply ran the remaining seconds off the clock with some dazzling ball-handling. The final buzzer sounded. Final score: 54–50.

Conference champs! Undefeated! Number 1 district seed!

The cylinder not firing and missing throughout the game was Bella. It wasn't that she was injured. She just did not seem to be with it. Her focus was lacking. Something was on her mind.

"What's wrong with you? You're not focused like before. Something bothering you?" Rey questioned Bella.

"I'm fine. Just gotta work through some things," answered Bella.

"Your definition of fine and my definition must not be anywhere near the same. You don't seem to have that fire anymore. That will to win just ain't there."

"The season's long. I'm just getting tired," Bella offered.

"You're in better shape than anybody. Don't give me that! What's eating at you?" Rey wasn't buying Bella's explanation.

"Nothing. I'm fine."

Rey was very concerned about Bella. She knew something was wrong but could not figure it out.

"You know I'm here for you, don't you?"

"I know. I appreciate it."

Rey decided to change the mood.

"Hey, it's Friday night. We just won conference, undefeated, secured first seed in the district tournament. Let's celebrate! A bunch of us are going to Cisco's for burgers and stuff. You coming? You could ride with me. Or do you have to meet Jamal?"

"No. He figured we'd probably want to do something if we won. So I'll go."

"Great! No practice tomorrow, so we can stay out as late as we want to. Well, at least till curfew. Have some big fun!"

"I'm ready," Bella said with a half-smile.

CHAPTER 17

Brayden was feeling very down and depressed.

"I've got to get away from there!"

"What's the urgency? Are you in trouble again?" Koen asked.

"It's home. I can't take it!"

"Does it have to do with you getting in trouble at school?"

"My dad's not mad because of what I was doing. He's pissed because I got caught!"

Brayden explained his family dynamics to Koen. Koen listened intently.

Brayden didn't know exactly how the counseling thing would pan out, but he sincerely hoped it would be able to lead him to some profound answers.

He was reluctant to talk to someone who was a complete stranger. But Koen possessed an ability to get people to relax and feel comfortable, confident, and assured. Brayden just opened up. He said many things that surprised even him. When his time was up, he felt like a different person. He had gotten so many things off his chest that had been weighing him down for so many of his young years. It wasn't anything that Koen said or did. It was just the release of pent-up frustration, anger, and disappointment.

As the counseling sessions progressed, Koen and Jolene began to feel more and more assured that the SMART program was an excellent venture and a positive service to the youth.

The client they were most impressed with was Brayden. He was 100 percent into the program. He found a new sense of self. Koen and Jolene loved his development so much they made him a peer leader. His growth was exciting to witness.

CHAPTER 18

Rey was extremely worried about Bella. Bella just wasn't herself, and Rey was very frustrated that she was not able to help her.

"What the hell is wrong with you? You better be freaking truthful! I'm tired of watching you mope around here in a daze. You don't care about anything! You don't try anymore. You are going to let your team down right when they need you most. We, as a team, are on the verge of doing something special. Making school history. But we can't do it without you! Look, I'm your best friend. If you can't trust me, who can you trust?" Rey was fuming!

"I'm fine. I—" Bella began.

"Stop it right there! Now you're starting to piss me off! You are not fine, and you know it. So knock it off! Spill it! Right here! Right now!"

Bella began to tear up. Her palms became sweaty, and her whole body started shaking. She knew Rey was dead-on. She knew she had to let it out, or it was going to consume her. But what about the consequences, the repercussions?

"I don't know...I can't..." Bella was reluctant.

"Whatever it is, it's eating you alive. I've only known you three or four months, but I know when something's bugging you. What is it, Bella? What is it?"

"It's not what. It's who."

"Who? Is it that pompous ass Jamal? Is that who it is?"

Bella immediately burst into uncontrollable almost-hysterical sobbing.

CHAPTER 19

At the Davis household, Tyler was once again screaming at Brayden.

"Boy, you're gonna have to get back to work!"

Brayden just sat there, staring out the window.

"Don't you hear me! Your dumb ass has cost this family a whole lotta money. So you need to get back on track and find a new place for business."

Still Brayden was nonresponsive.

"Hey!" Tyler screamed.

He slapped Brayden in the back of the head—a hard slap.

"You better answer me, boy! What you gonna do? You owe me! How you gonna repay me? Speak up, punk!"

Brayden's head was pounding. His vision was blurred. He stood up and turned to face his father and said, "I'm not repaying you anything."

"Excuse me?" a stunned-looking Tyler asked.

"You heard me," Brayden said.

"Why you ungrateful little—"

As Tyler swung, Brayden reached up and grabbed his arm. Holding it tightly, he looked directly into his father's eyes with a look that Tyler had never seen or ever expected to see.

Brayden sternly told his dad, "You will not hit me again! If you do, you will get that ass-whooping you've been deserving for at least the past seventeen years. Don't test me. I promise you, it won't be pretty."

They stood there, staring into each other 's eyes. Then Tyler looked away. Brayden let go of his arm.

"Get the hell out of my house! Don't you ever talk to me like that again!" Tyler ordered.

"I'll talk to you any way I please. I'm tired of being your little butt boy, your whipping boy. No more! I'm not going to be like Mom. I'm not going to let you make me into what you want me to be. I want better. I'm going to get better," proclaimed Brayden.

"You don't know better! All you know is sellin' dope. You've messed up school. You'll never be nothing more than what you are right now. Mark my word, you'll come beggin' me to let you start making money again."

"Think what you want. I'm through!"

Brayden turned and walked toward his bedroom. He stopped, turned around, and spoke.

"Why don't you want me to do better? Why don't you want me to get more out of life? Is it because you screwed up what you had, so now you want me to wallow in the same misery?"

Brayden waited for a response, but none came.

He continued, "Well, I've rolled in the mud long enough. I'm tired of being dirty. I can't and won't take it anymore. I will not let you break me. My change begins right here, right now. Where I'll go, I don't know. But wherever I end up, it'll be better than here. Hate me. Despise me. Loathe me. Whatever. The cycle must be broken. I love you and Mom, but I'm not going to live like this anymore. I just can't do it."

An unfamiliar silence fell upon the Davis household. Tyler would not look in Brayden's direction, yet Brayden somehow knew his words did not fall on deaf ears. He moved on to his room and packed a few essentials. On his way out the front door, he left a short note on the living room table.

Brayden had reached his limit. He was able to reveal to himself his inner strength, and he immediately knew what he could and would do.

CHAPTER 20

Elwood High School was at an all-time fever pitch. And why not? The girls' basketball team was undefeated and expected by all observers to go to state. The boys' team was no different. They had one early-season loss but steamrolled opponents from then on. Rey and Jamal were MVPs in their respective conferences and poised to, once again, be named first team all-state. This was going to be the best post season ever for Elwood.

That day was the big pep rally. The last two hours were filled with activities that delighted the one-thousand-plus students. There were treats, games, skits, competitions, team introductions, so on and so forth. Everybody in the school was in good spirits. Morale—staff and students—was at a level never before seen at Elwood High School. What a great day!

That afternoon was the last practice for both teams before the next night's games in the district tournament. The girls practiced in gym number 1 at the same time the boys practiced in gym number 2. Neither practice was as intense as normal. They just worked on polishing up some last-minute details. Even so, Bella still did not have a great practice. She still seemed to be distracted. Coach Mac pulled her aside to talk to her. That didn't seem to change her demeanor. At the end of practice, Coach Mac again called to her to hang back while the others went to the locker room.

"Bella, I don't know what's been ailing you, but you seem to have lost interest. I don't see that fire that was always there. I'm worried about you."

"I'm sorry, Coach. I'm trying to work through some things. My mind's been all over the place."

"Game time is tomorrow. You're not ready. I just want to let you know that you won't be starting. I've got a couple girls more focused and more into it than you. I'll put one of them in there in your place. I feel that would be in the best interest of the team," Coach Mac explained.

"I understand, Coach."

Bella knew Coach Mac was doing the right thing.

"I hope you get things straightened out soon, mainly for your sake. But we need the old Bella back. We can't do this thing without her. Understand?"

"Yes, sir."

"Go get changed."

Bella and Rey were the last to leave the locker room, as usual. As they walked out the door into the hallway, they saw two city police officers and three county deputies.

Jamal walked out of the boys' locker room.

"Jamal Brown?" Deputy McClain asked.

"Yeah?" answered a surprised Jamal.

"Drop your bag. Turn around, please. Hands behind your back," the deputy ordered.

Jamal was stunned. "What's going on?"

Deputy McClain responded, "You're under arrest. You have the right to remain silent…"

Jamal stood with an incredulous look upon his face as he was being Mirandized.

"What's the charge?" Jamal couldn't believe what was happening.

"We'll explain all that at county," Deputy McClain said.

Jamal's eyes met Bella's. His look was piercing, almost evil. Bella stared, looking shocked and afraid. She stood frozen as Jamal was led away.

With a touch to Bella's arm, Rey said, "C'mon. Let's go." Seemingly unconsciously, Bella walked out with Rey.

Carlos, Tiana, and Jacob had been waiting in the commons area for Jamal so they could hang out with him after practice was over. They were stunned. For once, Carlos was speechless.

Chapter 21

Brayden was at Koen and Jolene's residence.

"Thanks. I really appreciate it."

"No problem. We're here to help," Koen said.

Jolene added, "Have you had anything to eat this evening? You look hungry."

"To tell you the truth, I haven't eaten all day," answered Brayden. "I had too much on my mind."

"I'll get you a little something," offered Jolene.

She got up and left the room.

Koen continued the conversation. "Well, was it a bad afternoon?"

"Not as bad as I thought it would be," began Brayden. "I mean, he started in again with his yelling. He hit me, once. I flat out told him I'm done. No more hitting, no more selling. It's over. He was going to hit me again, but I caught his arm and told him that if he hit me again, I was going to kick his ass. That's when he kicked me out of the house. I really had nowhere to go. That's why I called you."

"That's why I gave you my number," Koen added.

Jolene returned with a tray holding two meaty sandwiches, a bag of chips, two thick and soft chocolate chip cookies, and a large glass of iced tea.

"Bon appétit." Brayden hadn't realized how truly hungry he was.

"So what are your plans? Have you had time to think about it?" Koen asked.

"Not a whole lot of time. But I do know I've got to help Mom get out of there. It won't be neat and tidy, but it's the only way. I just hope she'll understand."

"What about your dad?" asked Jolene.

"He seems to think he has molded me. So I'll just show him what he shaped me to be. It's the only way to get him out of the picture. He'll get what he deserves."

"Will you be able to live with yourself afterward?" Koen questioned.

Brayden replied, "I don't know. But I have to take care of business. It's the only thing that can be done to free Mom and myself from his cruel controlling attitude. I've got to do it."

For years, Brayden had despised the way his dad treated him and, especially, his mother. There was no free-flowing love in their household. Anything appearing to be caring or endearing was forced. So many times Brayden wanted to run away. But the fear of the unknown kept him there. So many times he wanted to be his mother's protector, but fear of a horrible beatdown kept him cowering in the next room, hoping that his mother would survive.

Tyler was not really a big man, but he was mean, truly mean. At times, it was as if Satan himself had taken over and was releasing his wrath through him. He had developed such an inner rage in an attempt to drown out the disappointment of throwing away a "made" life. He was in misery, so he wanted company.

Brayden, of course, had no choice. He was born into this predicament. From birth, home was hell. It never got better. The anonymous calls by neighbors to DFS did no good. The talks to school counselors did no good. The crying himself to sleep at night did no good. He felt that if he knew how to pray, prayer would not deliver him. He had grown to become so terribly pessimistic in regard to his family plight. Yet he dreamed of a better place and time. He dreamed of a day when he would free himself from the shackles of his family life and venture out, carving a safe and secure niche in which to prosper. He dreamed, all the while living in a nightmare.

CHAPTER 22

After practice, Rey went with Bella to Aunt Alicia's.

"They got him today, Aunt Alicia," stated Bella.

Aunt Alicia seemed relieved.

"I was hoping it would be soon, but that's a lot sooner than I expected," she said.

"Just as we were walking out of the locker room." Chimed in Rey.

"Right there in school? In front of a lot of people?" asked Aunt Alicia.

"Not a whole lot. Just us and a small part of his entourage," said Rey.

Aunt Alicia asked Bella, "Did he see you?"

Bella nodded slowly and said, "He gave me a look that I don't ever want to see again."

"Honey, I've been doing a lot of soul-searching," Aunt Alicia said. "I'm so sorry for not being there sooner, for not being more involved. With you trying to pick up the pieces of your life after having your parents stolen from you, I should have been more caring, more open, more understanding. I'll admit, I was more concerned about me than you. That was so wrong!"

"That's all right, Auntie."

"No, it's not! I was not there for you. There is no excuse for that. You really needed someone. I ripped you away from everything you knew. I was selfish. I felt robbed, intruded upon. I thought my life was ruined," Aunt Alicia confessed.

"Aunt Alicia, what's done is done. Believe it or not, what you did may have been a blessing. Oh, I was mad having to leave my friends, neighborhood, school…all that. I resented you. But I told myself, that's all right. I'm going to make it. I'm going to prove to her that I can do what I need to do to be all right."

"You are your parents' daughter. And that's a good thing," Aunt Alicia complimented.

"Thanks. But what happens with Jamal now?" Bella wondered.

"We have to let the courts do their thing," Aunt Alicia offered.

"How long will that take?" asked Bella.

"The wheels of justice turn rather slowly, so they say. Jamal will probably be out this evening. You know his dad is going to be pissed—oops! Sorry, Ms. Alicia. I forgot where I was," said Rey.

Aunt Alicia responded, "That's okay. I agree with you."

"Will I be safe?" asked Bella.

Bella was truly concerned for her safety. She had never been involved in anything remotely similar to this. She had come to fear the very individual she had, at one time, thought to be a godsend.

*****

Bella and Jamal seemed to be a great match. They had the same interests. They were both strikingly good-looking. They both loved the game of basketball and played it at a high level. Bella was a perfect lady, and Jamal seemed like a perfect gentleman. The operative word being *seemed*.

Jamal was used to putting on airs. He could charm most people without really trying. Once he got you in his hooks, it was, more often than not, too late. You were at his beck and call. Whatever he wanted, he got. It worked the same way with the young ladies. He would charm them, then swoop in for the kill. He felt that whatever he wanted, he should not be denied. Such was the case with Bella.

He was the perfect gentleman. He opened doors, talked respectfully, never too forward. This was the case for the first month of their relationship. Bella was smitten. She was drawn completely in. She felt Jamal was Mr. Right.

Things began to change. When he started questioning her about everything she did, everywhere she went, and every male she talked to, she thought nothing of it. Even when he would always put off meeting her Aunt Alicia, or the five or six times he got angry because she wanted to do something with Rey. Bella played it off as him being stressed and simply wanting to be with her. She thought she was in love and was convinced that he was just as in love with her. The true Jamal came to light the weekend they were to watch movies or play video games at Jamal's house.

The afternoon started out innocently enough. They ordered takeout from a local Cajun restaurant and took it to Jamal's house. Jamal's father, Mayor Deiondre Brown, was home. The three of them ate lunch together. Afterward Jamal and Bella went downstairs to the rec room. Bella was quite impressed with the setup.

"What do you want to do? Watch a movie or play video games?" Jamal asked.

"I'm so full right now. What about a movie?" Bella answered.

"Here's the collection. Which one?" Jamal offered.

"You pick. I trust your taste," Bella conceded.

Bella and Jamal sat on the soft cushiony sofa close to each other. As the movie played, Jamal put his arm around Bella's shoulders. A few minutes later, he began kissing her softly on her forehead. Bella smiled, thinking that was romantic. He grabbed her chin and kissed her on her lips. She kissed him back but began to feel a little uneasy. She began to feel vulnerable and trapped. And before she knew it, Jamal's hands were all over her body. She told him to stop. He kept on. She began to struggle, but she could not free herself. She started shouting and screaming. That did not slow her assailant.

After what seemed like an hour, Bella, exhausted from her frantic struggle to ward off Jamal's attack, lay sobbing on the sofa in a fetal position.

"Get yourself together! You can't be looking like this when I take you home," Jamal demanded.

"Why!" a tearful Bella asked.

"What do you mean why?" Jamal countered.

"Why would you do this to me!" Bella was shaking and shaken.

"I didn't do anything to you," Jamal contended.

"What! You tried to rape me!" Bella exclaimed.

Grabbing Bella by the throat with one hand, it was evident that Jamal was truly angered.

"Don't you ever say something like that again! I don't rape nobody! You brought that on. Case closed!"

Bella stared incredulously at Jamal. She was speechless.

"Don't be going around spreading no lies about me either. Nobody will believe you. I wouldn't go around talking 'bout us having sex. People might think you're pretty loose or something," Jamal warned.

"What!" Bella could not believe her ears.

"People would figure you wanted to get me in the sack to try to lay sole claim to me," Jamal proclaimed.

"You have got to be kidding me!" Bella was in shock.

"I would suggest you act just like you've always acted before. After all, you are the new girl. Who do you think people are going to believe? People know me. They trust me. They love me. What more can I say?" Jamal boasted.

*****

"As crazy as it might seem, you realize most people will blame you," Rey remarked.

"That's what Jamal said," recalled Bella.

Rey added, "For some reason, it seems everybody loves Jamal and thinks he can do no wrong."

Aunt Alicia jumped in the conversation. "I realize that. He's such a manipulator. He snows just about everyone." She paused momentarily before saying, "You know, I was thinking…"

"About what?" Bella asked.

"Well, he's a senior, right?" Aunt Alicia continued, "He's always been in the spotlight. Girls have always been attracted to him. With that being said, what's to say he hasn't done this before?"

"I had heard rumors of that going on. But don't you think someone would have reported that if it had happened?" asked Rey.

"Not necessarily," said Aunt Alicia. "Jamal and his family have status and influence. Status and influence can be very intimidating, especially to a young teenage girl. I would bet the farm this is not the first time."

"We'll probably never know, though. Nobody's going to talk. If they were scared before, they'll be even more scared now," Rey said.

"Bella, you are a trooper, a real heroine," Aunt Alicia commented.

"I don't feel like one. I just want to do what's right," Bella remarked.

"That sometimes takes extreme courage," said Aunt Alicia.

"Well, Bella, you are my hero," said Rey. "I really mean that." She hugged Bella. "I better get home. Dad will start to get antsy on a night before game day. You try to get some rest. Hey, if you take tomorrow off, Coach and everybody will understand. You do what you need to do. See you. Bye, Ms. Alicia."

"Bye, Rey, and thanks for everything. You've been a true friend. I couldn't have done it without your support. You're the best!" Bella acknowledged.

CHAPTER 23

Bright and early the very next morning, Coach King, head coach of the Elwood High varsity boys' basketball team, was in Dr. Earlis Cooke's office.

"Look, that's not fair to the student," pleaded Coach King.

Dr. Earlis Cooke inquired, "In what way is it unfair, Coach King?"

"Sounds to me like you've already decided his guilt," said Coach King. "You are convicting and punishing the kid before the courts have ruled on anything."

"That's not the case, Coach. According to district policy, a serious charge such as this must be fully investigated, and during the investigation, the alleged perpetrator may be suspended for a period of time as deemed appropriate by the administration."

Coach King was pleading his case. He could not believe what had happened. Eighteen hours ago, everything seemed perfectly poised and in position for a state run. Now his star was suspended and not allowed to participate in any school district activity.

"Can't you talk to the superintendent? Nothing has been proven. You are going to be damaging this kid," Coach King continued his plea.

"I have talked to the superintendent. And the school board. Our decision is long-term suspension until our investigation is complete. If the police served an arrest warrant, there must be something serious and a lot of probable cause involved. With that in mind, you can try your hand at talking to them, but I can assure you that nothing will change," Dr. Cooke informed the coach.

Coach King left Dr. Cooke's office with mixed emotions: shock, anger, confusion, frustration. When he had heard of Jamal's arrest, he was totally shocked. Never in his wildest dreams could he have envisioned such a thing happening. Even though he didn't really know the true scope of the incident, he was angry because he felt the administration was too harsh on Jamal, simply based on an accusation. He was confused and frustrated because in a matter of hours, he would be taking a perennial favorite into a district tournament, now minus its star, not knowing how the news of the incident had affected the psyche of the rest of the team. His lineup must be changed. His game plan must be altered.

His confidence was shaken. He wondered if that would be evident or noticeable to his players.

What a difference a day makes.

CHAPTER 24

Three Days Ago

After its briefing, the Buchanan County Drug Task Force departed, en route to the target location. They had never been to this particular residence, but they had been aware that suspicious activities had been observed there. Up to this point, there had never been enough reliable information available to execute a search warrant.

At 3:00 a.m., entry was executed, and the occupants were seized and detained.

This was to be one of the easiest warrants the task force had ever served. Everything was just as the confidential informant had said—where the occupants would be at that particular time of morning, where the cache of drugs and money would be, and the amount of each that would be found. The execution of the warrant yielded $20,000 cash, twenty pounds of marijuana, two kilos of uncut cocaine, one kilo of methamphetamine, a wide assortment of prescription and synthetic drugs, plus one very interesting item.

The informant had told the narcotics detective that the prize of the raid would be found in an upstairs closet in the guest bedroom. It would be hidden behind a false panel in the upper right back corner of the closet, wrapped in a plastic trash bag.

Sure enough, inside that plastic trash bag was something that was bound to shake the very core of the small community of Elwood.

CHAPTER 25

Game 1 of the district tournament was a breeze for the Lady Bulldogs. The number 1 seed versus the number 8 seed. Rey was at the top of her game, so were her teammates; all except Bella. She still was not at her best. She tried but just could not get her game back on track. Even so, the Lady Bulldogs rolled to a twenty-five-point victory.

The boys' varsity was in a dogfight all night long. Had it not been for two missed free throws with four seconds left in the game by the Janson Flyers, number 8 would have knocked off number 1. The number 1 seeded Bulldogs would have been sent packing. But they lived to fight another day.

"You're a big plus, Bella," Rey said.

"I don't know about that," answered Bella.

"Hey, you could have taken the night off. No, you show up, give it your best. Granted, it's not what we're used to seeing, but your effort was there. That says a lot," added Rey.

"I wish I could block all the distractions out of my mind. I try, but I can't," Bella lamented.

"Hang in there. Things will work out."

Bella could only say, "I hope you're right, and soon."

CHAPTER 26

Lametrius Brewer was a high-powered defense attorney. He was, by far, the best in the tricounty area. Everyone knew that whoever could afford his services, 98 percent of the time, charges would be dismissed, reduced to an infraction, or a flat-out acquittal. He played to win. At any cost. And he usually did.

Brewer drove his brand-new Lexus sedan up the long driveway, parking in the circle drive just to the left of the front door. He grabbed his leather briefcase, walked to the huge front entrance, and rang the doorbell. The door swung open. Standing there to greet him was Mayor Deiondre Brown.

Deiondre Brown moved to Elwood at the age of twenty-four, nineteen years ago. He and his wife, Camille, came here to live out their dreams. Before long, they were well on their way.

Both received their MBAs from the prestigious Columbia–Rockhurst University. They met in their junior year, fell in love, and married shortly after graduation.

They had immediately seen the immense business potential in the growing community of Elwood. Being young, energetic, and ambitious, it did not take the Browns long to become firmly entrenched in the business and commerce community of Elwood; he in retail and she in insurance. The ascension up the company ladders was swift. Within four years, they were both regional managers in their respective fields. They joined numerous community and volunteer organizations. They were an instant hit. Everyone was enamored with the young couple.

During their second year living in Elwood, the Browns were blessed with the birth of a beautiful healthy baby boy. Everything was just fantastic for them.

As the years progressed, so did the status and influence of the Browns. Camille was president of the area chamber of commerce as well as an elected member of the county council. Deiondre immersed himself in local politics from the very beginning, compiling a well-known track record and establishing a name of familiarity to voters. Such was instrumental in getting him elected to the mayoral office of Elwood at the age of thirty.

The Browns earned lots of money. They were able to purchase a brand-new ten-thousand-square-foot home in an elite neighborhood. Everything was moving along perfectly for them and their small family. Three years ago, things seemed to begin to unravel.

Camille was as honest as the day was long. She believed in keeping all her dealings above board, whether dealing with business and/or relationships. That was the major difference between her and Deiondre. He liked to fudge as much as he could get away with to gain an edge, to increase his personal profit.

At first, it was easy for Camille to overlook that aspect of his personality. As time went on, the fudging turned to flat-out dishonesty, and the dishonesty became harder and harder to tolerate. Camille warned Deiondre that his dishonesty, if it continued, was going to cause irreparable damage to their relationship. He ignored the warnings. He was too high on status, wealth, and influence. Camille honestly tried. But as they say, "It takes two to tango." Well, Camille found herself dancing alone.

The divorce was mostly amicable. They both had wealth, but Deiondre had more. They both had status, but he had more. They both had influence, but he had more. That caused the scales to tip heavily in Deiondre's favor in a community like Elwood, in a county like Buchanan.

"Mr. Brewer. Good to see you. Come in," Mayor Brown invited.

"Good to see you, Mr. Mayor. How are you?"

"I've definitely had better days," Mayor Brown said.

"I can imagine, sir."

Brewer followed the mayor down a long spacious corridor. They settled in a large recreation room. Even he was impressed with the setup.

"Can I fix you something to drink?" asked Mayor Brown.

"I'll take a bottled water, please," requested Brewer.

"You bet. I believe I'll have something a bit stronger, if you don't mind," Mayor Brown asserted.

"You go right ahead. Won't bother me in the least."

"As you are well aware, Mr. Brewer, my son is in a mess. I am interested in what you think, and I guess—first things first—if you would be interested in even taking the case," Mayor Brown said.

"So you want me to represent your son?"

"Yes, sir," Mayor Brown affirmed. "You're the best around, and I have faith in you."

"I appreciate that. Well, the first thing I'd like to know is all the particulars, every minute detail."

"Are you saying you'll take the case?"

"Mr. Mayor, I never would have darkened your door had I not wanted the case."

As he talked, he could see the cash piling up in his bank account.

CHAPTER 27

Four days after the Buchanan County Drug Task Force raid, Brayden Davis was in a visitor's meeting room at the Buchanan County Detention Center.

He sat nervously waiting. He didn't know how this meeting was going to go. While sitting, he reflected on what he had done. He wavered back and forth. On one hand, he thought he could have continued with business as usual. On the other hand, he strongly felt a need to take action, to make a change.

As the door opened, Brayden's heart began pounding in his chest. His palms became sweaty. A headache accompanied the heightened stress. At the door, hands and feet shackled, adorned in an orange jumpsuit, stood Hailey, his mother. She looked pathetic. She looked frail and broken, almost unrecognizable. Brayden could only feel sympathy. His eyes welled up. He got up, walked to her, and gave her a strong very heartfelt embrace.

They sat across from each other at a worn wooden table. For what seemed like several minutes, nothing was said. Finally, Hailey spoke.

"I'm sorry, son," Hailey apologized.

"You have no need to apologize, Mom."

"Oh, yes I do. For all those years of being involved in this mess."

"Mom, you had no choice."

"Yes, I did. You know I did," Hailey said. "I was weak. I still am. I knew what could happen. I even allowed you to be put smack-dab in the middle. I've been here before, but not this deep. I'm really scared, Brayden. Very scared."

"I understand, sort of. I was scared out of my mind when I got arrested. But thank God, a way was presented to me to be able to right myself. The same will happen for you. I know it will, Mom. I know it will."

"I don't know, son. This is pretty bad. I don't see any way out of it. Why? Why did I stay so long? After I read the note you left the day your father threw you out, I kept telling myself it was time for me to go too. I kept thinking it, but I never acted on it. I actually had packed some things and put 'em in the basement. I just couldn't leave. I was too scared. I just couldn't leave," Hailey spoke, looking down at the table between them.

"I know it may not be the best of situations right now, but you are finally out of there, Mom. You don't ever have to go back. Ever!"

"But I'm going from one hellhole to another. At least at home, I knew what to expect. Now I have no idea. I'm really afraid, Brayden."

"It's going to be all right, Mom."

"They knew everything, Brayden. The police. They knew where to find everything. They even knew right where the book was. The cash. The stash. Tyler always talked about being so careful. I don't understand."

"Don't worry about that now," Brayden told her. "Let's just think about you surviving your time in here. That's the most important thing."

"I don't know if I can!"

Hailey doubted her own strength and toughness.

"You can and you will. Mom, promise me this. If they come to you with a deal, seriously consider taking it. No matter what. Promise me."

"I don't know, son."

"Mom, you have to. It may be the only way to save yourself. And I need you to save yourself."

"I don't—"

"Please, Mom. I'm begging you. If you won't do it for yourself, do it for me. Please?" Brayden begged.

There was a long pause.

"I will try, honey. I will try," Hailey promised.

An officer entered and informed them that visitation was over. Both acquiesced. Brayden watched as his mother shuffled out of the room, looking as though she was taking a final stroll to an unwanted ending to a troubled confused life. Brayden realized that she had no idea, no clue, as to how all this came to be. He wanted to tell her but felt it wasn't the right time. He hoped she would understand.

CHAPTER 28

The district championship game was about to begin. The Lady Bulldogs were primed and ready to go. The semifinal game reinforced a message to all who were watching—this is the year of the Bulldogs. They steamrolled to victory, 84–25. They were once again firing on all cylinders. Rey was pure Rey, and more importantly, Bella was back. It was great to see. It was evident in her walk, her intensity and tenacity. She and Rey were the perfect complement.

Their opponent for the championship game was the Janson Flyers. The Flyers had lost just two games all season; one was to Elwood. Ever since that game, the Flyers had been on a mission—to avenge a loss they felt never should have happened. They got their wish, a rematch. What's that saying, "Be careful what you wish for"?

Bella Seger was a woman possessed. Something seemed to click within her that catapulted her skill level to heights she had never experienced nor had anyone ever witnessed of her. Rey was momentarily taken aback. Just momentarily.

The crowd was treated to the *Rey and Bella Show*. It was a sight to see.

The Janson Flyers were never in the game. The score at halftime was 62–12. The second half was given to both teams' subs. Final score: 84–30. District champs! Two out of three season goals had been achieved. There was one more to go.

The Bulldog varsity boys didn't fare as well. They never made it to the championship game. The loss of Jamal Brown was too much to overcome physically, but more so mentally.

Coach King was a wreck. He could not hide his lack of confidence in his team. They knew he did not believe in them. They responded the only way they felt was appropriate—playing with a lack of confidence. They were demolished in the second round of the district tournament by a team they had easily handled twice during the season.

What a difference one player can make.

CHAPTER 29

Elwood was about to enter into the most bizarre string of events in the history of its existence.

The prosecuting attorney of Buchanan County, Jordan Luzier, was inundated with paperwork sent his way from the sheriff's department. Report after report, complaint after complaint, all dealing with one particular individual and that individual's indiscretions. All the complainants wanting to pursue charges.

In the weeks following the arrest of Jamal, rumors and speculation spread rampantly. All the talk and innuendo evidently was enough to spark an outpouring of rage, disgust, and, probably most importantly, courage.

There were a total of twenty-five young females, ages fourteen to nineteen, who came forth alleging they had been sexually harassed, assaulted, or raped. The incidents spanned a period of four years.

Prosecutor Luzier realized he was dealing with a sexual predator. However, this was not your typical defendant. This was the son of one of the wealthiest most influential men in the state. This was the beloved superstar and most sought-after athlete in the state's history.

Was all this real? Surely all these females couldn't be fabricating such horrendous accusations. Is there really a monster hidden behind that Adonis-like facade? Is it all he-said-she-said evidence? Will they all be willing to testify? So many questions. So few answers.

Not only did PA Luzier have to prepare to prosecute Jamal, but he had to simultaneously prepare a solid prosecution against Jamal's father, Mayor Deiondre Brown.

The Buchanan County Drug Task Force had discovered a ledger during their raid on the residence of Hailey Crawford and Tyler

Davis. The ledger did not have full names written out. It was mostly initials and first names. The initials appearing most often and most noticeably were that of MDB. The first entry in the ledger dated back ten years, "MDB/7-14/2P/Ma."

Understandably the task force members had no idea who this individual, or any other, might be.

CHAPTER 30

Meanwhile, the Elwood Bulldogs girls' team continued its march to the state finals. They easily handled their opponents in the sectional and quarterfinal rounds.

The semifinal matchup pitted them against the number 1 ranked team in the state, the Hazelton Eagles, two-time defending state champion, seventy-five-game winning streak, and five-returning starters. What was obvious from the start was that the Lady Bulldogs were not intimidated, not even slightly impressed.

The Hazelton Eagles had never run across a team that operated with such precision and all-out never-relenting intensity. The speed. The tenacity. The athleticism. Bella and Rey were masterful. As the Bulldog fans clapped, screamed, and shouted, all the Eagles fans could muster was, "Wow!"

The championship game two days later was even easier.

The Lady Bulldogs—undefeated, conference champions, district champions, and now, *state champions*! The trifecta of titles. The pinnacle of high school athletic success.

Bella was ecstatic! She had never been a part of something so exciting. Number 1 in the state! No doubt about it! And she knew she was an important part in the success of the journey.

Amazing! Awesome!

What was also amazing, exhilarating, and totally unexpected, Bella found herself named as an all-state first team selection, along with her teammate Reahlin.

CHAPTER 31

Ten Days Later

Koen asked Brayden, "How are you getting along?"

"I'm doing okay," he answered.

"Hey, I've got someone I would like you to meet."

"Oh yeah? Who might that be?" Brayden asked.

"First of all," Koen began, "let me tell you that I don't normally do this kind of thing. But it just seemed so right."

"And?" Brayden started to feel a little nervous.

"There's this young lady—"

"Hold on!" Brayden interrupted. "Wait a minute. Where you going with this?"

Koen, smiling, explained, "Well, I kinda thought you two might get along rather nicely. She's very good-looking, great personality, smart, athletic, and relatively new to the area. She's going through a rough time, and Jolene and I thought maybe you would be someone who could help her keep her world somewhat on an even keel."

"How can I do that when my world is all upside down and turned inside out?"

"You're getting your act together. Everything is starting to slow down," Koen added.

"My parents are both in jail. Things are slowing down? Doesn't seem like it to me," Brayden replied.

"You knew that was an eventual possibility. It just may have happened before you expected it to. The authorities finally caught up with them. That's on them, not you."

"Not necessarily," hinted Brayden. "Let me let you in on a little something."

Brayden divulged some pertinent information and details to Koen. Afterward the two waited patiently—Brayden not so much—for the arrival of the aforementioned female.

Brayden was a somewhat shy individual when it came to the opposite sex. He had never really dated. He would go places and hang out in a group, never one-on-one. He had had crushes on several girls, but they never knew it. He admired them from afar. He didn't have a close friend to confide in. It was just him and his thoughts. He never felt he was astute enough to carry on a seemingly intelligent conversation with a female by himself. *What should I talk about? What if I say something stupid or goofy? What if she wants to talk about something I know nothing about?* All those thoughts have run through his head before, and here they were, racing through his head again at breakneck speed.

"Relax, man. Everything will be fine. Joe and I will be here. This is just an introductory get-together. No pressure," Koen assured Brayden.

"Right! That's easy for you to say," said Brayden. "This is new to me. I've never done this before."

"Don't worry about it. Just be yourself."

"I'll try. Man, I'm really nervous," confided Brayden.

"Understandable."

The doorbell rang. Jolene answered the door. In walked the most beautiful young woman Brayden had ever seen. Now he was petrified.

CHAPTER 32

It was not until the drug task force investigators sat down with the confidential informant were they able to fully identify the individuals associated with the initials.

The author of the ledger was Tyler Davis, Hailey's common-law husband and Brayden's father. For someone who had dropped out of school and who always looked so disheveled and aloof, he kept very meticulous records. According to the informant, Tyler never missed recording a transaction, be it picking up a package or dropping off a package.

In this ledger were the names/initials of some of the most prominent local and regional men and women. Not only were the names/initials in there, but alongside were dates, descriptions, amounts, and totals.

Names/initials listed:

> SSJ—Sgt. Steve Johnson (member of the Elwood City Police Department)
> BD—Brayden Davis
> HD—Hailey Davis
> KB—Katherine Bauman (state representative)
> JD—Janice Declue (county assessor)
> ME—Mitchell Eaton (manager of the Elwood Walmart)
> JB—Jamal Brown
> JE—Jacob Eaton (son of Mitchell and good friend of Jamal)
> MDB—Mayor Deiondre Brown

The drug task force did its best to keep everything quiet about the ledger, but to no avail.

As most people know, the purpose of law enforcement is to serve and protect. Those who enter into the profession become a part of a semisacred brotherhood. They take pride in their solemn oath. They take pride in their duties and responsibilities. They become their brothers' keeper. They watch and cover their brothers' back. They demonstrate an extraordinary high degree of integrity and morality. Unfortunately not all sustain such exceptional professionalism.

As in many, probably most, professions, there are those who operate with low regard for ethics, whether innately or influenced by a seemingly irresistible temptation. Such was the case in the Buchanan County Sheriff's Department.

Jase Estes began his career in the Buchanan County Sheriff's Department at the age of twenty-one, working as a 911 dispatcher. Within two years, he was attending the law enforcement academy offered at nearby Johnson Community College. He graduated top in his class. He appeared to be well on his way to a stellar career as an officer of the law.

True to form, Deputy Estes exhibited exceptional skills in the field. There did not seem to be a situation he could not handle. His actions were quick, swift, and by the book. His fellow officers had nothing but praise for him. His ascent up the promotion ladder was fast, by all accounts. Within five years, he was a sergeant in a department of three hundred male and female officers, and he was in line to be promoted to lieutenant in the next few months. He was reliable, dependable, and trustworthy. He didn't make mistakes until—

Sgt. Estes was a fun-loving guy. He got along with everybody. Even those he arrested and sent off to prison thought of him as a great person. They never spoke ill of him. Sgt. Estes always had a smile and a joke. The citizens of Buchanan County, young and old, all knew him and thought of him as a true server and protector of their community. He gave law enforcement a good name. He was like the local Superman. Well, as we all know, Superman does have his kryptonite.

Two Years Ago

Sgt. Estes had just participated in a luncheon and was standing in the reception area of the hotel. He was approached by a woman who he had noticed at the same luncheon seated across the room from him.

She was a very attractive woman. She appeared to be in her late twenties to early thirties. She was of medium build, 5'5" tall, shoulder-length brunette hair, and beautiful hazel eyes, outlined by very stylish eyeglasses.

"Sgt. Estes, I am Jaylyn Reese. It is an honor to meet you."

"It is my pleasure to meet you," replied Sgt. Estes.

"I have heard so much about you, all good, of course," Jaylyn went on. "And now I finally get to meet and talk to our local hero."

"You're starting to embarrass me now." Smiled Sgt. Estes.

"That's not my intention. I'm just stating facts."

"Well, I'm no hero. I am a server and protector," offered Sgt. Estes.

"It's my understanding that you are the best at what you do," added Jaylyn.

"I just always try to do the best I can do."

Sgt. Estes was clearly interested in Ms. Reese.

"Is that at everything?" she asked.

"Yes, ma'am," he assured.

"I know this might seem a little forward," Jaylyn said, "but would you like to have dinner some time? I would really like to get to know more about you."

"That doesn't sound like a bad idea. Then by the same token, I could get to know more about you," Sgt. Estes countered.

"That's a deal. Here's my card. I hope to hear from you soon," Jaylyn said with a huge smile and a sparkle in her eye.

"You can count on it," guaranteed Sgt. Estes.

Kryptonite comes in a multitude of forms.

CHAPTER 33

Prosecutor Jordan Luzier was assessing the case against Jamal Brown with Assistant Prosecutor Connie Stephens.

"We've got twenty-five alleged victims, correct?" asked Assistant PA Connie Stephens.

"That is correct," replied PA Luzier.

"The problem is we have nothing but he said she said. Their word against his. We all know how that would play out," Assistant Stephens added.

"That is true."

"And you are not concerned?"

"I didn't say that," answered PA Luzier.

"Well, you sure look and act like you're not worried."

"Looks can be deceiving," said PA Luzier. "Besides, I can't let my opponent see me sweat."

As far as Assistant Prosecuting Attorney Stephens knew, all the testimony and evidence they had to date were the victims' words versus the words of the accused. In a county so entrenched in an atmosphere where wealth, power, and influence reigned supreme, this particular defendant would surely be acquitted.

PA Jordan Luzier was concerned, but not about that particular aspect of the case. He was more concerned about the security of information concerning witness testimony and evidence. He knew of the leaks and illegal behaviors of some of the once-trusted members of the law enforcement community, even members of his own staff. He did know, however, that Assistant PA Stephens was beyond reproach. Luzier just believed that at this particular point in time, what she didn't know wouldn't hurt her.

"I've got some angles I'm working," continued PA Luzier. "When I get a firmer grip on a strategy, I will sit down with you, and we can decide if it is the best way to proceed. Right now I need you to recontact the first twenty girls on the list. See if their stories are the same, that no details have changed. Make sure they are still willing and able to testify and that they are aware of the stressors involved. I will do the same with the remaining five on the list."

"No problem. I'll get right on that. Do you think I should inquire of each if there's been any outside pressures to change their minds?" asked Assistant Stephens.

"By all means. I would not be surprised to find out that most have already been approached in some form or fashion."

CHAPTER 34

Brayden sat next to the bed, holding his mother's hand. He was worried, mad, disappointed, and mistrusting. He kept wondering, what if she had heeded that note he had left on the living room table the day he left home:

Mom,

I can't take it anymore. I will not be back. You have got to get out of here, and fast! Please leave! This is not a good place for you. If you don't get yourself out, I'll have to do it, and it won't be pretty. Mom, I love you!

Brayden

Hailey had read the note over and over. She knew Brayden was right. She knew she needed to leave. But every time she started to walk out that door, some unexplainable force stopped her in her tracks and made her feel guilty for even considering such a move. This happened time and time again. She was too weak to fight the force working against her.

Hailey now lay in a hospital bed in Elwood Memorial's ICU, barely clinging to life. She was the victim of a stabbing while she was preparing to shower one morning in the Buchanan County Correctional Center. What was thought to be a homemade shank had just nicked her aorta. She had lost a lot of blood, but miraculously, she was hanging on.

What was so strange about the incident was the fact there were no witnesses to the attack despite there being ten female prisoners and three female guards in the immediate area. Also the weapon used was never recovered.

Brayden knew what all this meant, yet he couldn't fully comprehend. As he sat there with tears rolling down his face, he whispered, "Mom, you're gonna make it. And I'm going to make sure that the ones who did this will pay. They will pay dearly. Count on it!"

CHAPTER 35

"Aunt Alicia, I had something strange happen to me today at the library," Bella related.

"What's that?"

"Well, some lady came up to me when I was looking for a magazine..."

"Hey, aren't you Bella, the one who played basketball for the Lady Bulldogs?" asked an unknown female.

"Yes, ma'am," Bella answered.

"Congratulations! You girls had one great season," the unknown lady said.

"Thank you. Yes, we did." Bella smiled.

"That must have been some great feeling."

"Oh, it certainly was. I had never experienced anything like that before. It was awesome!" Bella was once again feeling that sensation of elation.

"That sounds like it was quite exciting. Congratulations again. Wow, Elwood has all kinds of excitement going on. I guess you've heard about the charges against that young man?" the unknown female added.

"What young man?" Bella asked.

"Jamal Brown," said the unknown female.

"Yes, ma'am," Bella said.

"That's a shame. He's an outstanding young man. Don't you agree?" the unknown lady asserted.

"Well..." Bella hesitantly responded.

"I bet you it's just a couple jealous, envious teenage girls trying to make trouble because he wouldn't date them," the unknown female implied.

"I don't know..." Bella was starting to feel very uneasy.

"These young girls need to learn to keep their mouths shut. Ruining someone's reputation could have serious consequences. You know what I mean?"

"Umm..." Bella wanted to leave this lady and this conversation.

"They probably don't realize who they are messing with," the unknown female continued. "You, on the other hand, seem like you're a pretty smart girl. If you happen to know who any of them might be, maybe you could tell them that it would probably be in their best interest to drop everything and just move on with their lives. Otherwise it could get ugly. Oh, well. Hey, it was nice talking to you. Again, congratulations."

"Nice talking to you. Thanks again," an uncomfortable Bella replied.

"Who was the lady?" asked Aunt Alicia.

"I don't know. I'd never seen her before," said Bella.

"Would you be able to describe her or identify her if you saw her again?"

"I'm quite sure I could," Bella said confidently. "She was very attractive and stylish. I saw her leave, but I couldn't tell what kind of car she drove. What do you think she meant by what she was saying?"

"I think it's quite obvious what she meant. Be sure to tell Mr. Luzier about that when you see him later today," Aunt Alicia suggested.

"Most definitely," promised Bella.

CHAPTER 36

Things were starting to heat up in Elwood. All the big players in Elwood society were sweating bullets. Word was starting to get around that a good number of bigwigs were in trouble, big trouble. Everyone around was aware of Jamal Brown's situation. They were aware of what he was accused of. Ninety-five percent believed he was innocent or that the charges would be dropped, and he would never see the inside of a courtroom. Jamal himself believed he would never be found guilty of any type of crime.

The day he was arrested, almost before he arrived at the Buchanan County Sheriff's Department for booking, his bail was posted. He was released from custody but court-ordered not to attend the high school due to the anxiety it may cause the alleged victims. Jamal was to be instructed through Elwood's homebound curriculum studies.

One might think that a predicament such as this would damage the ego of an eighteen-year-old teen. Not Jamal. As a matter of fact, his ego seemed to be bolstered. He didn't shy away from public attention. He was seen regularly around town—at the mall, the grocery store, restaurants, the fitness center, etc. He was never alone. He was always flanked by his father and a very imposing male figure and, of course, his usual entourage of Carlos, Tiana, and Jacob.

The public did not shy away from him either. People clamored to him wherever he was. It was as though he was some Hollywood celebrity. The public seemed not to be able to get enough of Jamal, and he was loving every minute of it. After all the rumor and innuendo floating around about this young man and the horrific crimes he had supposedly committed, the public seemed to love him even more. Or did they? Was it actually the young man they loved? Or was it the wealth, power, and influence he represented that was so endearing to them?

What was most shocking about this overwhelming public display of affection and support for an accused sexual predator was the fact that most members of the families of the victims were in Jamal's corner. How demoralizing that must have been for the victims. They were trying to step up and do the right thing, yet they can't get support from those closest to them, those that are supposed to love them above anyone or anything else; those they are supposed to be able to rely and depend on during the most difficult of times.

Wealth, power, and influence can make an excellent potter out of one who wields such.

CHAPTER 37

"According to one of the members of the task force, a lot of people are in trouble," informed Sgt. Estes.

"What for?" asked Jaylyn Reese.

"Well, it appears there was some ledger found during a drug raid."

"What's that got to do with anybody?" Jaylyn wanted to know.

"Supposedly it is filled with names, dates, transactions, all of that."

"Still, I don't get it," Jaylyn said. "Who did the ledger belong to?"

Sgt. Estes said, "Tyler Davis."

"What! He kept a ledger!" Jaylyn could not believe it.

"Evidently."

"Unbelievable! But knowing him, it is probably a jumbled mess."

"On the contrary," reported Sgt. Estes. "it is very detailed and orderly. Our friend's name is plastered all throughout."

"What friend?"

"Who do you think? Friend number one. The one you got me involved with."

"Oh, I see," said Jaylyn. "What are you going to do?"

"I'm working on something," said Sgt. Estes.

"What?"

"It's not necessary that you know the particulars. The less you know, the better off you are."

"I understand."

"How did the appointment go?" asked Sgt. Estes.

"It went really well. Young people today are so simple and naive. I almost feel sorry for them," Jaylyn told him.

"I wouldn't underestimate those young ones. Some of them are pretty slick, you know. They make you think you got over on them, and the next thing you know, it's vice versa."

"I'm not worried about that. I've been at it a lot longer than they have. I work my magic pretty well, don't you think?" Jaylyn teased.

"I would have to agree. It works well with me."

Sgt. Estes could not deny her magic.

Since their meeting two years ago, Sgt. Estes and Jaylyn Reese have been together. It worked out much differently than either had originally planned.

Ms. Reese's services had been procured to entice Sgt. Estes into a lucrative business deal. That she did. But she found that she herself had been enticed and reeled in by the suave smooth-talking Sgt. Estes.

Sgt. Estes was genuinely interested in the very attractive Ms. Reese. His initial intent was what it had always been with women—love them, then leave them; never let one tie you down. Ms. Reese had something special. After their first dinner date, Sgt. Estes was hooked.

They were recognized as the beautiful couple of Elwood. They had good looks, wealth, and huge influential status. They were the most sought-after couple. If there was to be an important event in Elwood or the immediate surrounding area, it was validated by the presence of Sgt. Estes and Janet Reese.

They were living the high life and loving it.

CHAPTER 38

Lametrius Brewer was spending a lot of time in his office. His para-legals were working overtime. He knew he had his work cut out for him.

He had studied over and over what the prosecution had as far as their case against Jamal Brown was concerned. He sincerely believed his client had little to worry about. He knew that with his keen defense skills, he would more than likely get the charges dropped. If not dropped, his client would go to court and surely be acquitted. There was no physical evidence. Everything was their word against his. He couldn't understand why the prosecution would even present such a weak case to the court.

Brewer had never gone up against PA Jordan Luzier. The only thing he knew was how good he himself was and how intimidating he was to opposing attorneys. He had a reputation that spread far and wide. Everyone knew he was the best around. He believed PA Luzier would be just as impressed and, most assuredly, just as intimidated.

Maybe Brewer was justified in his thinking. This was, by far, the biggest, most high powered, high-pressured case ever tried by the young prosecutor. His previous prosecutorial experience had dealt with traffic offenses, DUIs, misdemeanor assaults, petty thefts, etc.; nothing that would compare to the magnitude of the scope of these proceedings.

Even for an experienced prosecutor, the task ahead would seem foreboding. Yet PA Luzier was unflappable. He worked with an air of assurance and confidence that was somewhat baffling and confusing to most members of his staff. They could not understand how he could be so cool, calm, and collected in such high-stress situations. That was just his makeup.

From the moment he entered this confusing, complicated, mixed-up world, he was laid back, never making a fuss. Extremely intelligent. Very observant and analytical. Always thinking three or four steps ahead. An uncanny ability to read people accurately and completely. Attributes he would most certainly need for the tasks ahead.

CHAPTER 39

"How you doing this evening?" Sgt. Jase Estes asked.

"Not too bad. How 'bout yourself?" came the response from Lt. Marcus Riney.

"Never been better. I hear you guys have been quite busy."

"For sure. That last bust really yielded a boatload of treasures, which translates into a boatload of paperwork. That's the nature of the job," continued Lt. Riney.

Lt. Riney and Sgt. Estes had developed a strong friendship years ago. Sgt. Estes was Lt. Riney's FTO (field training officer). Through that experience, the two formed a deep bond.

Lt. Riney was second-in-command of the Buchanan County Drug Task Force; young, energetic, and driven. He too was a fast climber through the ranks. His hard-charging no-nonsense approach got him prominent details and quick promotions.

Being of the same ilk made it easy for the two to relate to each other. They hung out together on a regular basis, usually at their favorite watering hole, P & E's.

"So when will you finally come over to the dark side?" asked Lt. Riney.

"Man, I've told you already. That full-time drug work just ain't me. If I run across something every now and then, fine. But every day would be too much. Besides, them drug people are crazy," Sgt. Estes said.

"Well, you would fit right in," joked Lt. Riney.

"Whatever."

Lt. Riney inquired, "Are you and your lady going to the cabin anytime soon?"

"I don't know for sure. We've got some free time this weekend, and no plans. Hard telling what we'll end up doing," was Sgt. Estes' reply.

"I would suggest a trip to the cabin," said Lt. Riney. "Santa left you an early Christmas present."

"Oh really?" Sgt. Estes really perked up.

"Santa knew you really wanted this. So he figured you shouldn't have to wait. Santa's cool like that. It's put away in a nice secure place," stated Lt. Riney.

"I like early Christmas presents. So does Jaylyn. We'll just have to take a short ride this weekend. Need another drink? I do."

Sgt. Estes ordered a couple more drinks.

CHAPTER 40

Mayor Brown was talking to his son Jamal. "You remember that we have a meeting today, right?"

"Yeah, but I thought maybe we could do something else instead." Jamal was not interested in attending any meeting.

"Son, this meeting is pretty important."

"I know. But we haven't been out of this house in a week. At least I haven't," Jamal complained.

"Hey, I know it's tough on you, being cooped up like this," sympathized Mayor Brown. "But we really don't have a whole lot of say in the matter. The trial preparations are winding down, and we don't want to be put in a situation that might complicate things or jeopardize our chances."

"You said we don't have anything to worry about."

"And we don't, son. But people have a way of stirring up trouble just because. By staying away from them, they don't have the opportunity."

"Look, Dad! I need some fresh air! I need to get out and see people! They need to see me! I'm important to them! I ain't worried about any haters! There's too many that love me."

After thinking intently for a few seconds, Mayor Brown said, "You're probably right, son. I'll see what I can do."

From a young tot, Jamal always got his way with his dad. His mother tried to discipline him, but Dad always bailed him out. That was one of the major wedges that caused the split between Deiondre and Camille Brown. No matter what indiscretion Jamal committed, Deiondre was right by his side, fixing things, covering things up, telling him, "Don't worry about it." Little wonder that as Jamal grew older, he came across as arrogant, spoiled, narcissistic, egotistical, so on and so forth.

Jamal didn't really have a true friend. He was too much into himself. The people that hung around him were into his status and not into him as a person. They just wanted to be included in his "celebrity" circle. But he couldn't see that. Or could he?

CHAPTER 41

It was early May, and Elwood was getting really busy. High school graduation was in a couple weeks. The city's Mayfest was coming up during the Memorial Day weekend. Plus the biggest court proceedings in the history of Buchanan County were set to begin on June 1.

Bella was getting excited and anxious. She was full of excitement because she was graduating and looking forward to going off to college to study forensic medicine. She was anxious because she was the key witness in the case against Jamal Brown. She had held up well under such grueling and agonizing stress.

Bella had been fortunate to have had a strong support system surrounding her. Aunt Alicia had been unbelievably stalwart. Rey had been there every step of the way. Plus Bella didn't have to feel like a lone victim. There were seven other young women ready and eager to testify, to tell their story, to unburden their minds.

Bella had another avenue for release. She had a beau. She had fallen head over heels for this young man. It wasn't like her time with Jamal. This was entirely different. There was no need for posturing, no need to be pretentious, no feeling like walking in someone's shadow. Bella felt like she could really be herself. Brayden made her feel alive and free. Ever since the evening she walked through the door at Koen and Jolene's, she had been enthralled.

Brayden, once he overcame his *petrification*, was immediately smitten. Surprisingly to himself, he was able to carry on a pleasant, meaningful, and prolonged conversation.

That initial meeting was all it took to have Brayden and Bella become inseparable.

CHAPTER 42

Assistant PA Connie Stephens met with Hailey Crawford, who was still in the hospital.

"We really appreciate you taking the time to talk to us. We know you've been through a lot and have a long recovery moving forward."

Hailey said, "I just figure it's time I grow up and get some backbone."

"Now you know, if it gets out that you were talking to me, you might be in line for another attack," warned Assistant PA Stephens.

"I know. But I figured you guys could prevent that from happening," Hailey acknowledged.

"How's that?"

"Maybe I watch too much TV or something, but you've got to protect me. Please?" Hailey was pleading. "I have a lot of information. I know about a lot of different things and a lot of different people. I'm willing to tell you everything I know. But you've got to keep me safe. I can't go back to that jail. I just know they will finish me off."

"We have been thinking along the same lines. We have made arrangements for protective custody. Once you are released from here, we will put you up somewhere safe and secure," guaranteed Assistant PA Stephens.

"Oh, thank you. Thank you. I'll tell you everything I know. Everything!" Hailey was so grateful and relieved.

Assistant PA Stephens asked, "What made you want to do this?"

Hailey stated matter-of-factly, "Near death and my son. Mainly my son."

CHAPTER 43

It was a nice Saturday afternoon in May. The sky was partly cloudy. There was a nice soft breeze blowing. The temperature was hovering around sixty-seven degrees.

The gazebo area of the park was crowded with well-dressed well-wishers and a small wedding party. It was the day that Koen and Jolene were to be joined in holy matrimony.

In attendance were Koen's mother, Kaneisha; Jolene's parents, relatives, and friends from Memphis; the couple's coworkers and their significant others. Even that new fresh young couple, Brayden and Bella, was present to join in the joyous occasion and festivities.

As Koen stood in the gazebo with the minister and watched as the wedding party marched in, he scanned the crowd. He spotted his many relatives on his mother's side. He saw his many friends and coworkers. But he did not see the one face he was hoping to see. He was disappointed, yet this is what he had expected. His father was too busy to take time out to be a part of this big momentous, once-in-a-lifetime happening. Koen thought of how if his father was not the center of attention, or if something was not orchestrated or put together by him, it wasn't worth his time. Such was the makeup of Lametrius Brewer.

Any disappointment or anger Koen might have been feeling quickly disintegrated when he viewed his gorgeous bride walking down that carpeted lane toward him. The sight of Jolene filled Koen with peace, joy, and, most of all, love. All seemed right with the world.

CHAPTER 44

That same Saturday afternoon, Sgt. Jase Estes and Jaylyn Reese hit the road. They were en route to their cabin getaway.

"Tell me again why you decided to hit the road this weekend?" Jaylyn wanted to know.

"I never said. It just seemed like the thing to do."

"I'm not buying that," Jaylyn replied. "You are not the impromptu, spontaneous type. You have to have a plan."

"You know me too well," Sgt. Estes conceded.

"So once again, why are we going to the cabin?"

"Don't be so inquisitive. If I told you the reason, it might be spoiling a very romantic event."

"Really? I guess I should trust you then. I wouldn't want to spoil a romantic surprise." Smiled Jaylyn.

"No, you wouldn't."

Sgt. Estes really had no reason to keep Jaylyn guessing. He was just having some fun at her expense. He knew that the early Christmas gift from Santa would excite her just as much as a romantic surprise, maybe even more.

CHAPTER 45

In recent days, it had come to the attention of Lametrius Brewer that a pretty damaging piece of evidence existed that could really cause a problem for his client, Jamal Brown. He had discussed this fact with Mayor Brown.

"In light of that piece of evidence, I was wondering what your thoughts are," said Brewer.

"What do you mean?" queried Mayor Brown.

"It will be tough to rebut that evidence," Brewer continued.

"Can it be done?" asked Mayor Brown.

"I'm sure it can be."

"Well, whatever it takes. I have every bit of confidence you will figure it out."

"Just wanted to get your thoughts on it."

An agitated Mayor Brown exclaimed, "We want our day in court! The prosecutor is not going to try and intimidate us with some stupid pieces of evidence! I don't care what he has. It will not hold up. And I'm paying you to make sure it doesn't!"

"Whoa! Settle down, Mayor. I'm just making sure we're on the same page."

"I'm sorry. Just a little stressed."

"Understandable. Just relax. We'll get this taken care of."

"I can help you in any way you need," assured Mayor Brown.

"I know you can, and that's what I'll be counting on."

CHAPTER 46

Bella and Brayden were sitting around Aunt Alicia's, trying to catch their breath from the frenzied activities—past, present, and upcoming.

"So many things are going on. We had the wedding this past weekend. Graduation is in a few days. The trial will begin in a couple of weeks. This is so much," Bella noted.

"I know. It always seems like everything has to happen all at once," Brayden agreed.

Bella admitted, "Sometimes I wonder how I'm going to be able to handle all this. Can I handle all this?"

"You can handle it all. You are a very strong young lady. Think about one thing at a time," Brayden advised. "Graduation is very important, and it's up first. Put your focus there. Savor that experience. It's a once-in-a-lifetime experience. Once it's over, then you can move on to the next thing."

"I know that's what I should do. But it's so difficult."

"Do you think we should back off from each other for a while?" asked Brayden. "Maybe give you a little more breathing room?"

"No way!" Bella objected. "If not for you, I would have probably lost it by now. You, Aunt Alicia, and Rey are my rocks. I need you."

"I was hoping you'd say that. I feel the same about you. We've both got some very tough, stressful days ahead of us. Together we can do it. I know that. I believe that."

"Speaking of, how's your mom? Have you talked to her recently?"

"Just the other day. She's recovering, slowly but surely. I still worry about her. They still have a guard in her hospital room, but I'm still scared for her. I don't know, maybe I watch too much TV. I just think she is in a lot of danger."

"What about your dad?"

"What about him?"

"I was just wondering if you knew anything about his condition or status," Bella said.

"Not that I care," said Brayden, "but he supposedly refuses to cooperate. That's fine. He'll get exactly what he deserves."

"Let's hope. You know how the wheels of justice are sometimes greased."

"I vowed to my mom that I would see to it that these people would pay, and I won't stop till it happens," Brayden proclaimed.

"I'm with you. No matter what. My mom and dad always told me, 'Never shy away from the truth, no matter who is standing in front of you trying to change your thinking,'" said Bella.

"I bet you had some pretty awesome parents."

"You have no idea," Bella said with a smile and a tear.

CHAPTER 47

Tyler Davis had been enduring his incarceration by battling through bouts of anxiety, fear, trepidation, and loneliness. He's had one lone visitor throughout his stay, his attorney, David McLaughlin.

McLaughlin visited Tyler at least once a week. As he traveled to the jail, he wondered which Tyler he was going to meet with that day. Would it be the nervous, fidgety, hand-wringing Tyler, or the cowering, soft-spoken, ultraparanoid Tyler.

Tyler's main concern was whether he would live to see his court date. He knew that he knew a lot of dirt on a lot of big-name people. He could ruin a lot of people. Would they trust him to keep his mouth shut? Or would they make sure he kept his mouth shut? Those two thoughts occupied his mind 24-7. He barely ate or slept. He stayed away from the general jail population as much as possible.

Attorney McLaughlin had spent the majority of his visit times trying to reassure Tyler that everything would be all right and that he was safe in jail. Tyler was not buying it. Tyler found it difficult to talk about his case and how McLaughlin could best represent him. His conversation was focused on how to protect and preserve his life. McLaughlin had the unenviable task of putting together a defense for, in all actuality, an uncooperative client.

Tyler's mental state had not been helped by his knowledge of what had happened to Hailey. Ever since, he'd been feeling that his days were numbered. Though he had a strange way of showing it, he really cared for Hailey. He had been agonizing over her plight.

Tyler just wished one of those big-name people would come visit him so he could assure them he would stay quiet. Even in such a fragile state of mind, he knew he could be trusted. But could he really?

CHAPTER 48

All the major players in the biggest happenings in the history of Elwood were busy planning, plotting, and preparing. They were keenly aware of how life-altering the outcomes would be for not only them but for the entire communities of Elwood and Buchanan County.

The mayor, Deiondre Brown, was fighting to keep his political and social status and influence.

The high-powered defense attorney, Lametrius Brewer, was looking to keep his reputation and unblemished record intact.

The young laid-back prosecutor, Jordan Luzier, was desiring to see justice meted out, even if it involved the wealthy and powerfully influential.

The misfits, Tyler Davis and Hailey Crawford, were simply wanting to live.

The arrogant and cocky Jamal Brown was looking to return to business as usual—doing what he wanted, when he wanted, to whomever he wanted.

Low-key youthful Bella Seger was wanting a quiet, smooth, uneventful normalcy to return to her life.

The once-troubled Brayden Davis was looking forward to a long-awaited freedom for him and his mother.

Different individuals. Different lives. Different expectations. Common events yielding uncommon results. As with us all in life, we seem to be living and following very different and unique paths. Yet one event, or series of events, can reveal how intertwined we actually are. Such was the case with the people of Elwood and Buchanan County.

Just a year ago, everything was status quo. The wealthy and influential were operating in their seemingly impenetrable members-only bubble, without a care in the world. The lower tiers of local society just trudged on, looking to maintain or hoping for a positive uptick to their current circumstances. The only concerns of the youth were fashion, social media, grades, boyfriends/girlfriends, sports, and video games.

Time has a way of shifting things.

CHAPTER 49

Prosecuting Attorney Jordan Luzier was busy putting the finishing touches on his opening argument in the case of the *State of Kansas v. Jamal Maxim Brown*. The jury selection was complete. The big event was about to begin.

Many people wondered why there was not a change of venue for the proceedings. Most felt it would be impossible to get a conviction with a jury comprised of Buchanan County residents. Too many people were either fans of Jamal or were, some way or another, under the influence of Jamal's father, Mayor Brown.

PA Luzier was well aware of the talk, the skepticism. Yet he was undaunted. He firmly believed the jurors selected from the pool of Buchanan County residents would be fair, unswayed, unintimidated, and would see that Lady Liberty would not be blinded or the scales of justice unbalanced. Others were not so sure.

PA Luzier's confidence was bolstered by one particular piece of evidence. He was certain it would lead to a conviction once it was presented to the jury. As a matter of fact, he was quite surprised that he had not gotten a call from defense attorney Brewer wanting to talk about a plea deal. But then again, as he thought more about it, he realized the people he was dealing with would never concede defeat. They always felt they could overcome any potential threat to their protected, supposedly untouchable, status. PA Luzier also knew they would go to any lengths to preserve that aura of invincibility.

There was a knock on his office door.

"Come in."

In walked senior law clerk Rhonda Kinder.

"Sorry to disturb you, but this is important," began Rhonda.

"What seems to be the problem?"

"I just got a frantic call from the sheriff's office. What they said is disturbing."

PA Luzier didn't have to hear the details. He knew it would happen.

CHAPTER 50

"It's been a while since we've been to our weekend getaway," commented Jaylyn Reese.

"That it has. Are you missing it?" responded Sgt. Estes.

"Kind of. Especially after that nice little surprise you had for me on our last trip there. That was quite amazing!"

"I'm always aiming to please."

"You certainly did that time, above and beyond. I'm still wearing that smile. You are amazing! Did I say that already? Well, twice is not enough. You are *amazing!*"

The power couple of Elwood and Buchanan County was relishing in its seemingly good fortune—financial security, community notoriety, and a growing sphere of influence. They were loving life and each other. With all the turmoil and hubbub going on around them, they appeared undaunted. It was as if the outside world had nothing to do with their world; as if worry and strife had nothing to do with their existence, as if the biggest proceedings to ever hit Buchanan County were of no concern to them.

"Are you going to stop by the first day of the trial tomorrow?" asked Jaylyn.

"No, I probably won't. I've got some other things that I need to be doing. What about you?" responded Sgt. Estes.

"I was thinking about it. I thought it might be good to make a showing, just to let my boss know I'm thinking about him and his family."

"Probably a good idea. Then maybe we could meet up for dinner afterward."

Jaylyn agreed, "Let's plan on it. I've been wanting to try that new restaurant, Smokee Mo's Bones. It sounds delicious!"

"It's a date," confirmed Sgt. Estes. "Just call me when you get out of there."

Undaunted, unfazed, oblivious, or too arrogant? Only time would tell.

CHAPTER 51

It had been three months since the jailhouse attack that was intended to snuff out the life of Hailey Crawford. She survived, barely, and now sat in a comfy chair in the living room of her new temporary residence; a safe house, two counties removed from Buchanan County. She was not alone.

With her was Samantha Pope. Sam, as she was called, was Hailey's 24-7 roommate. She was also a detective with the KBI, Kansas Bureau of Investigation. Her charge was to comfort, protect, and record any information Hailey wanted to give about the drug operation Tyler was part of.

As Hailey had lain in that hospital bed, recovering from the stabbing, she thought about her life, over and over. She wondered why it turned out to be so tumultuous.

She did not have a bad life as a child. She was born into a medium middle-class family. It was a two-parent household. She was the youngest of four children. Both parents worked but were very active in their children's lives.

They were excellent parents. The kids did not lack love, attention, or quality time. Their house was adequate, clean, comfortable, well kept. The Crawford family was well thought of in the community.

School was not a chore for the Crawford children. All four were very bright and studious. Each of them was at or near the top of their respective class academically. It was smooth sailing until Hailey's seventh-grade year. Things began to change for her.

Hailey became inattentive at school. She began to show signs of irresponsibility in all aspects of her life. That brilliant mind she possessed, she refused to use. She became argumentative, rebellious, untrustworthy. To her, her parents were always wrong. Arguments were plentiful. For four solid years, her parents gave it everything they had. They reached out to every available outlet and organization in an attempt to right the ship of their sinking daughter. Nothing worked.

Hailey eventually dropped out of school. She, as could have been expected, began getting in trouble with the law. One of those incidents got her involved with Tyler Davis. She had been trapped ever since.

"This is something I should have done a long time ago. Why did it take me going to death's door to finally open my eyes? I've been a real dummy."

"I don't think so, Hailey. Look at it this way, some people never open their eyes. You got caught up. Choices and circumstances put you in a bad way. It's just taken you a while to decide to change things," offered Sam.

"A long while. I guess late is better than never." Reflected Hailey.

Hailey was finally waking up.

CHAPTER 52

Jamal and his father were having dinner together at Hacienda El Dorado, the swankiest restaurant in a four-county area. They didn't seem to have a care in the world.

Mayor Brown began, "I see that you are still in good shape as far as your homebound grades are concerned. That means there are a lot of colleges still very interested in you."

"That's what I like to hear," countered Jamal.

"Have you narrowed down your choices?"

"For the most part. Four of them really interest me. One is KU, of course. They need a scorer. Plus it's close to home. All my local fans could make it to a lot of games. The others are quite a ways away—Indiana, North Carolina, and UCLA."

"Sounds like good choices. Do you think the workouts and personal training are helping?"

"It's keeping me in shape," Jamal continued, "but I need to be playing. Competition is what I thrive on. I love to dominate."

"I know, son. Once you commit, you'll get all the playing you need. You've got to be patient. Once we get this court crap over with, everything will be back to normal."

"Yeah, I know. By the way, did you get that one thing taken care of?" inquired Jamal.

"Of course! You have nothing to worry about. That which is lost will never resurface," boasted Mayor Brown. "That calls for a toast."

He discreetly poured a portion of his bottled wine into an opaque glass and slid it to Jamal. They picked up their respective glasses, brandished huge smiles, and clanked away.

The world was their oyster, so they believed.

CHAPTER 53

The crowd began assembling three hours before the courthouse doors were to open. It had the appearance of a Walmart on Black Friday having a fifty-inch HDTV on sale for $100. Everybody wanted to get in.

Security was ramped up. There were law enforcement personnel from various jurisdictions—state, county, and local.

Media outlets were well represented. All the major newspapers sent their best reporters. The three major national TV companies' regional affiliates set up broadcast sites. Since TV cameras and photography were banned inside the proceedings, sketch artists had paper and pencils at the ready. The big-time had hit Buchanan County.

It wasn't something the citizens necessarily wanted, but they were in the spotlight. Their quiet existence was no more. The world would be watching, scrutinizing the proceedings, delving into their personal lives, dissecting their community and how it operates, passing judgment—warranted or not.

Once the doors opened, the District 1 Circuit Courtroom filled to capacity in a matter of minutes. People from all walks of life were there. Though there was no reserved seating, the who's who of Elwood and Buchanan County were seated in the front rows. All others seemed to take their places accordingly, filling the main floor and balcony seating.

It's funny how that works.

The opening arguments got underway.

Prosecuting Attorney Jordan Luzier began, "Ladies and gentlemen of the jury, what we have here is a classic case of wealth, power, and greed. Those who have it all thinking they can control, mold, and shape those that have less. Those who have it all thinking they can have whatever they want, whenever they want, from whomever they want. Those who have it all attempting to make those with less feel like they are less of a human being. This is a classic case of 'My name is so-and-so. You must do what I say. You better keep your mouth shut. I can do what I want, and nothing will happen to me. No one will believe you.' This is a classic case of manipulation, intimidation, and bullying.

"We have a young man born into a family of wealth, influence, and power. A young man raised in privilege, given everything he wanted, whenever he wanted. A young man raised with the mindset that the world was his, and he could do what he wanted, whenever he wanted, to whomever he wanted. A young man that was never required to be accountable for his actions. A young man sheltered from any significant consequences for his actions. A young man who was raised to believe that Daddy will take care of it, no matter what happens. This young man is the defendant, Jamal Maxim Brown.

"Ladies and gentlemen, you will hear testimony from numerous witnesses detailing the horrendous nightmares they were put through at the hands of this defendant. You will hear testimony painting a picture of how, for the past four years, the defendant has been a prolific sexual predator. You will hear evidence of the fear and intimidation the defendant relied on to keep his depravity under wraps.

"This defendant may be young and an outstanding athlete, but he is a monster. Any female he sets his sights on is in extreme danger.

"Ladies and gentlemen of the jury, I thank you in advance for your service and attentiveness."

Judge Jameson directed. "Mr. Brewer, we will hear your opening statement at this time."

Lametrius Brewer offered his opening remarks. "Thank you, Your Honor. Good morning, members of the jury. I don't have a long drawn-out opening statement because it's not necessary. The reason I say that is because there is no evidence the prosecution can offer to verify or substantiate the testimony of the accusers. All you are going to hear is 'he said, she said.' There is no video. There is no audio. There is no eyewitness. There is nothing. Once again, 'he said, she said' thrown out by jealous, jilted, wishful girls trying to be a part of this young man's world, and since they can't be, they are trying to destroy his image and future, trying to bring him down to their level, trying to thwart his success. No evidence, just empty hurtful accusations. Thank you."

Judge Jameson ordered, "Mr. Luzier, the prosecution may call its first witness."

The high drama had begun.

CHAPTER 54

Talk of the trial was everywhere. At the end of the third day of testimony presented by the prosecution, people really started to take sides. Most believed Jamal would not be found guilty because no physical evidence had been introduced. Though most had sympathy and empathy for the young girls testifying, it was felt their words simply would not be enough.

Discussion and debate were taking place in the packed confines of P & E's Lounge. The drinks were flowing, and the talk and noise were nonstop. In the crowd were Sgt. Jase Estes and Lt. Marcus Riney.

"Have you checked out any of the trial yet?" inquired Lt. Riney.

"Actually I haven't. I've been quite busy with a couple other things. What about you?" replied Sgt. Estes.

"Not yet. I'm giving it a couple more days. Maybe the crowds will get smaller. I hear it's all been the same stuff day after day. I figure next week will get more interesting if what you're telling me is true."

"For sure, next week will be exciting. I'll bet big bucks on that," assured Sgt. Estes.

The two continued with small talk for hours.

Lt. Riney continued, "How's the mayor holding up?"

"According to Jaylyn, he is on cloud nine. He is superconfident that his son will be acquitted. She says there are a lot of accusers but no reports of the incidents when they happened, no visits to hospitals, no rape test kit evidence, nothing but their words. She says she doesn't even understand why the prosecution even filed charges."

"Maybe the PA wants to make a name for himself," suggested Lt. Riney. "He's trying to take down the mayor, the mayor's family, and half of the other local officials. Looks like somebody's looking for their fifteen minutes of fame."

Sgt. Estes retorted, "Well, he'll probably get his fifteen minutes, but it won't be for what he thinks. I think he's underestimating the mayor or overestimating his own expertise. Not to mention, he's going up against the best defense attorney around. Doesn't make sense to me."

"Yeah, I bet Brewer is just laughing at these proceedings."

"Jaylyn says he is more relaxed than she's ever seen him, and that's saying something. He's barely made a peep. You know, he's too good for them. I almost feel sorry for 'em." Chuckled Sgt. Estes.

"Good thing for early Christmas," said Lt. Riney.

"A toast to early Christmas gifts," offered Sgt. Estes.

A clank of beer bottles, and the small talk continued.

CHAPTER 55

"I think that is all that I know or, at least, can remember right now. Will any of that help you?" Hailey wanted to be useful.

"Immensely," affirmed Sam. "You've given us some very valuable information. The next question is, will you be able to get on the witness stand and tell it all to a jury?"

"That's what scares me. But you know, I believe I can do it. No! I know I can! I know I will! My days of being afraid are over," asserted Hailey.

"You know what? I believe you. You're a good woman, Hailey. A strong tough woman. You're not alone in this. You've got to remember that."

"I know. Do you have any kids, Sam?"

"No, I don't."

"Well, when you do, always keep in mind that your children can teach you a lot. Be open to that. Don't think that you are the only one that's doing the shaping, the molding. My son has been trying to help shape me for a long time, but I didn't pay attention. I resisted. Instead, I stayed under the spell of Tyler. I let him turn me into a formless, voiceless nothing. I had no true identity. I was what he told me to be. I accepted that for more than half my life. I did whatever he told me to do without hesitation, without question. The only time I worried was when it came to Brayden. I wanted him to be safe. I didn't want him to turn out like me. When he got arrested, I cried. I cried because I thought he was just like me—weak, unable to break from the hold Tyler had on us. I was wrong.

"You know, when he left home, I cried again. Probably harder than I've ever cried before. But this was a different cry. The tears were tears of joy. He did it! He did what I wanted to do but didn't have the courage to do. I was so happy for him. I was so proud of him. He was his own man. I thank God for that. God gave him what I couldn't."

"Don't sell yourself so short, Hailey."

"I'm just tellin' it like it is, Sam. Just tellin' it like is."

CHAPTER 56

Day six of the trial in the *State v. Jamal Maxim Brown* continued.

"You may call your next witness, Mr. Luzier." Directed Judge Jameson.

"Your Honor, the state calls Isabella Seger to the stand."

The moment had finally arrived. Bella had prepared herself for this. At least she thought she had. All the confidence-building she had done, all the prepping she had done with the prosecutor's office, all the support of Aunt Alicia, Rey, and Brayden, all the prayers, all those things seemed to be of no consequence at that moment. When her name was called, she immediately felt alone, scared, lost, and small. It was like the whole world was going to be watching, and she would look like a big fool. Lacking any confidence, she took the witness stand.

Strangely, though, when she raised her right hand to be sworn in, everything changed; a great weight was lifted. She knew exactly what she needed to do, what she wanted to do, what she had to do. She looked at the defendant with resolve. He shot her a menacing glare and somewhat of a smirk. This did not faze Bella. She knew the power was with her.

At the same moment, Mayor Brown had a sense of heightened tension. If this testimony went just like all those before, he would be truly confident that his son would be acquitted. There would be no way the jury would convict with no physical evidence. No way. This particular witness would be crucial. The tension was heightened, but the arrogance was evident.

"Would you state your full name for the court?" requested PA Luzier.

"Isabella Renee Seger," she responded.

After several more introductory, identifying questions, PA Luzier continued, "Ms. Seger, do you know the defendant, Jamal Brown?"

"Yes, I do."

"How do you know the defendant?"

"We were classmates at Elwood High School."

"Were you just classmates?"

"Up to a point."

"What do you mean by up to a point?"

"Well, we started out as friends, and then we began dating each other," explained Bella.

"How much time was it from being friends to dating?"

"I would say probably two to three weeks."

"Whose idea was it to take the relationship from friendship to dating?"

"It was a mutual decision."

PA Luzier continued, "So you felt it was a good idea to date the defendant?"

"Yes."

"How long did you date him?"

"About a month."

"A month. Why just a month? Was there something that happened that caused a stop to the two of you dating each other?"

"Yes, there was."

"And what was that?"

"He tried to rape me."

"Objection, Your Honor!" interrupted Defense Attorney Brewer.

"Sustained," replied Judge Jameson.

Without missing a beat, PA Luzier continued his line of questioning. "During the time the two of you dated, what was he like? In other words, how did he treat you?"

"He was very good to me. He opened doors for me. He bought me nice gifts. He talked nice to me and around me."

"Did he take you out to nice places?"

"Yes."

"Did he always pay?"

"Yes, he did."

"Would you use the word *gentleman* to describe him when out on a date?"

"Yes, I believe so."

"Were the two of you ever alone on a date, not out in public?"

"Only once."

"And when was that?"

"On Saturday, December 13, of last year."

"It seems like you have a vivid memory when it comes to that date. Correct?"

"Yes."

"Can you tell the court the details of that day that caused such an indelible imprint?"

Bella began recounting the events of that horrible day. Though it was painful, she maintained her composure and told every charming nice detail, as well as every frightening sordid fact.

"So are you telling the court that the defendant that you described as a 'gentleman' out in public turned out to be anything but that when he got you alone?"

"Yes."

"Are you sure your memory is correct?"

"Yes, I am sure."

"Are you sure it wasn't someone else?"

"I am sure."

"Were you dating anyone else at the same time?"

"No, I was not."

"Do you have any other proof that the events you described as happening on Saturday, December 13, of last year actually occurred as you say?"

"Yes, I do."

"And what might that be?"

"It is a phone recording."

Lametrius Brewer and Jamal sat up a little straighter. Mayor Brown's blood pressure soared.

"A phone recording? What do you mean?" Quizzed PA Luzier.

"My cellphone recorded the whole incident."

The entire courtroom became very silent and attentive.

Bella continued, "I had my cell phone in my back pocket, and somehow my video recorder came on and stayed on."

"The infamous butt dial," quipped PA Luzier. "The state would like to offer into evidence state's exhibit 1A."

Walking toward the judge's bench, PA Luzier held high in his hand a cell phone.

Mayor Brown was livid. He leaned over the front railing directly behind Brewer. Visibly shaken, he demanded, "Object to that!"

"I can't!" Brewer retorted.

"What do you mean!"

"They'll know something's up!"

"The jury can't hear that! Do something!" Mayor Brown demanded.

"Excuse me, Your Honor," interrupted Brewer. "I'm not sure we received this audio recording in discovery."

"Mr. Luzier, was this piece of evidence disclosed and given to the defense in the discovery stage?" asked Judge Jameson.

"Yes, Your Honor, it was. I have a receipt here depicting what evidence was delivered to and received by the defense. It was received and checked off by Mr. Brewer's investigator, James Daniels. Mr. Brewer should have a copy of this receipt because one was made at the time of delivery. I would figure it to be in his files somewhere," answered PA Luzier.

Judge Jameson questioned, "Mr. Brewer, is this correct?"

Shuffling through a pile of papers, Brewer answered, "I am checking, Your Honor. I can't seem to find it here. Will the court allow a short recess for me to contact my office to verify the receipt?"

"The time is getting late in the day," Judge Jameson countered. "It's almost four o'clock on a Friday. The court will stand in recess. We will reconvene at nine o'clock sharp on Monday morning. The jury is free to leave at this time."

Once the jury exited, Judge Jameson pounded the gavel, and the bailiff announced, "All rise!"

CHAPTER 57

There was chaos in Lametrius Brewer's office. Tensions were high. A lot of swearing, a lot of shouting, a lot of worrying.

"What the hell is going on, Brewer!" yelled Mayor Brown.

"You're asking me?" Brewer retorted.

"Damn right I'm asking you! How did they get that! How did they have that!"

"Once again, you're asking me!"

"Dammit, Brewer! Are you not my son's defense attorney?"

"I am indeed."

"Then what happened? How did you let this happen?"

"Wait a minute, Mayor."

Brewer was getting pretty perturbed that the mayor was pointing an accusatory finger at him and him alone.

"If I'm not mistaken—and I know I'm not—I told you about this. You implored me to do something about it. I told you I would need help. You—you, Mr. Mayor—assured me it would be taken care of. I trusted you that it would. You even affirmed that it had been taken care of over a month ago! So I don't know why you're trying to say it's my fault!"

"Did you prepare for this?"

Brewer was fuming.

"Prepare for it? There was supposed to be nothing to prepare for! How do you prepare for nothing!"

"I thought you knew what you were doing! Big-time attorney!"

"You know what, Mayor, kiss my ass!"

All Jamal could do was sit there, wide-eyed, nervous, and afraid. For the first time in his life, he had a sense that his dad was not in complete control of a situation, that his dad had not delivered on a guarantee, that his dad wasn't going to be able to keep him from accountability.

An interesting weekend lay ahead.

CHAPTER 58

"How did I do?" asked Bella.

"You did great. You couldn't have been a better witness," replied PA Luzier.

"Are you sure? At the end, I got kind of confused as to what was going on."

"Don't worry about that," assured PA Luzier. "They were a little confused and scrambling."

"So after you play the recording, will the defense attorney begin asking me questions?"

PA Luzier thought for a few seconds before answering. "Normally that would be the case." Pausing again, he continued, "But truthfully, I don't think you'll have to worry about that."

"Why wouldn't I?" Bella was not understanding. "I figured the defense is going to try to tear right into me and try to tear apart that recording."

"As I said, normally that would be the case. But things are a little different this time."

"You're getting us all out of whack here, Mr. Luzier." Chimed in Aunt Alicia.

"Probably." Smiled PA Luzier. "It'll have to stay that way for a while. At a later date, I will fill you in completely."

"Just trust Mr. Luzier like you have from the start. He's been spot-on from the very beginning," encouraged Brayden.

CHAPTER 59

"Do you think they're bluffing?" Jaylyn Reese seemed quite concerned.

"They have to be," answered a calm Sgt. Estes. "I have to give it to Luzier, though. He's craftier than I expected, but his little antics aren't going to work."

"How can you be so sure he's bluffing?"

"I just think he was trying to see what kind of reaction he would get from Brewer. I bet he expected a sense of panic. Instead, Brewer was cool and calm. Luzier has nothing, and he knows it."

"That's what I was thinking," added Jaylyn. "I just didn't know if someone had slipped up."

"Not a chance," reassured Sgt. Estes.

There are times when we entrust others to carry out an assignment and know, beyond a shadow of a doubt, they can be counted on to do what is needed and expected. Time and time again, they have come through. Until the very end, they will have our undying faith and trust.

CHAPTER 60

Early on Sunday morning, Koen and Jolene were getting ready for church. They both were just about finished when Koen's ringtone began sounding off. It took him a while to locate his phone. He raced to get it from the computer room.

After a few short minutes, Koen returned to the master bedroom, staring down at the phone in his hand. He stood there, silent.

Jolene noticed the incredulous look on his face. "What's wrong, hon? Who was it?"

Koen continued to stand in silence, still staring.

Hoping to get a response, Jolene asked, "Is everything okay?"

"Everything is just fine," Koen finally, quietly, responded.

"Who was calling?"

CHAPTER 61

Tyler Davis had been doing his best to keep up with the Jamal Brown trial. He had a sense that the outcome of that trial would hint to the outcomes of the upcoming trials involving the elite of Buchanan County.

He had been locked up for months; still his attorney had been his only visitor. There'd been no message nor messenger; nothing from anyone to assure him everything would be all right. There hadn't even been a message or messenger sent by anyone to threaten him to keep his mouth shut. That he would have welcomed, just because it would have let him know somebody was thinking about him. As it stood, it was as if nobody cared a lick.

Tyler had had so much time to think. Too much time. All the thinking was about to make him crazy.

Look at me. How did I get here? Why did I make the choices I made? How is Hailey? Does she ever think about me? Will I ever see her again? Will I ever get out of jail? What made me do what I did? Does anyone even care about me? Why doesn't anyone visit or write? Are they going to come after me to shut me up? Do they trust me? What should I do? Do I keep my mouth shut? Do I try to save myself? Why did I throw my life away? Can I, or will I, gain my life back? I've got to change. But I can't change. This is me. This is all I know. I'm scared. I want to help. I can't help. If I talk, it will be the end. If I don't talk, it will be the end.

Twenty-four seven. That's all that ran through Tyler's brain. He couldn't eat. He couldn't sleep. The same thoughts. One right after the other. Over and over. Day and night. Week after week. It was maddening, pure psychological torture. But no one took notice of his mental and emotional upheaval.

CHAPTER 62

A phone conversation between Mayor Brown and Jaylyn Reese:

"I need to see you immediately!" exclaimed an extremely excited Mayor Brown.

"What's the problem?" asked Jaylyn. She had never heard such a frantic tone in the mayor's voice.

He screamed, "You haven't heard! Where have you been?"

"Easy. Easy. No, I haven't heard anything. At least, I don't think I have."

"I need to see you immediately!" he insisted. "It can't wait until tomorrow. It has to be now!"

"Okay. Okay. Give me about thirty minutes. I'll see you then." She hung up with a quizzical look on her face.

"Who was that?" questioned Sgt. Estes.

"It was Mayor Brown. He's in some sort of a dilemma. He wants to see me right away."

"That guy's always been high-strung. He's probably fretting over nothing. You know how he gets."

"I know, but this time it sounds different. I just need to get over there and see what's up."

"Well, I guess so. After all, he does pay you the big bucks for advice. Just be careful. Call if you need me."

"Will do. Love you." She kissed Sgt. Estes and headed out to meet Mayor Brown.

Chapter 63

Brayden, staring into the eyes of Bella, said, "I just can't believe how amazing you are."

"What are you talking about?" asked a blushing Bella.

"Everything you do is extraordinary. You're a straight-*A* student. You're an exceptional athlete. You are fearless. You stand up to the most powerful, influential people in the county, and you don't even bat an eye. I want some of that character."

"Gee, thanks. I truly appreciate the compliment. But you've already got more than enough character. What you are about to do is super courageous. Don't downplay your own strength and courage. Give yourself your just due."

Here were two teenagers thrust headlong into situations neither one wanted to be in. Yet they never felt a need to shy away from, nor refuse to do, their moral duty. Two teenagers expressing mutual admiration, extolling the virtues of the other, not self-absorbed. Standing proud and unmovable. Standing for right. Standing for truth. Refusing to be intimidated.

One may wonder how two young people could have been so convicted, so courageous, so steadfast. What did they possess that so many that were twice their age did not possess?

CHAPTER 64

Koen arrived at El Hombres restaurant in neighboring Greene County around 6:00 p.m., about a half hour before the agreed-upon meet time. He was curious, anxious, and concerned. He had expressed to Jolene his desire to find out what was so pressing and important that his father wanted to meet him for dinner and talk. It was something in the tone of his father's voice that piqued Koen's curiosity. Ordinarily he would have blown his father off. But this was different.

At 6:20 p.m., Lametrius Brewer strolled into the restaurant. If something was bothering him, it didn't show in his walk or on his face. His stride, posture, and smile were as confident and cocky as ever.

The two shook hands. Brewer sat at the table with his son, Koen, to dine and converse.

"Koen, thanks for meeting with me on such short notice," began Brewer.

"No problem. What's on your mind?"

"A lot. A hell of a lot. I just don't really know where to begin."

He paused, as if searching for the right words or the right starting point.

"Something must really be bothering you," interjected Koen. "I've never known you to seem to be at a loss for words."

"Yeah, I know. The big high-powered defense attorney not knowing what to say. Pretty strange, huh? Well, here goes—"

But before he could begin, the waitress stopped at their table to take their orders. After a couple of minutes of idle chitchat and a rundown of the day's specials, the two placed their orders, and the waitress went on her way.

"Koen, you know my story. You know I've always been a very driven person. I've always expected the best. I've always wanted the best. I always had to have the best. I couldn't, I wouldn't, settle for less. My push for the so-called best eventually pulled me away from the best things that ever happened to me in my life—your mother and you."

"It's taken you all these years to come to that conclusion?" asked Koen.

"No, son. I came to that conclusion many years ago. But I didn't want anyone to know it. You see, I had built this reputation of being a tough, hard-nosed, no-nonsense, take-no-prisoners attorney. I felt I had to uphold that persona, even with my family. It cost me dearly. I have a great professional reputation. I've made lots of money. I have many fine expensive things. But in the quest for all that, I've had to pay a high price. Right now, I'm tired of paying. I've had enough."

"What are you getting at?"

"I want to get back to reality." Brewer went on. "The real world, the real things that matter, the real people that matter. I know it's going to take some time because I took myself a long ways away. But I've got to use that same drive and determination I had to take me here to take me back, to bring me back."

"This is all well and good, but what's this got to do with me?" questioned Koen.

"It has a lot to do with you. Son, you are a wonderful upstanding young man. You and your wife do an outstanding job at the counseling service. You are top-notch, and I'm going to need your services."

"Oh, I see. So you need help for a client."

"No, that's not what I said. I said I am going to need your services."

"You? That's interesting. Why would you need our services?"

"Once I tell you this next part, you'll understand."

CHAPTER 65

Jaylyn Reese was frantic. "We have to get a hold of Lt. Riney! This is important!" exclaimed Jaylyn.

"What are you talking about?" asked a surprised Sgt. Estes.

Jaylyn continued her rant, "Just what I said! You have to call Lt. Riney right now!"

"Wait a minute! It's almost midnight! Plus I don't even know if the man is working or what!"

"It is imperative that we find out if he did what he was supposed to do!"

"Hey, now! You need to get a grip! The mayor has gotten you all worked up."

"How can you be so calm and so sure your buddy did the right thing? The mayor is really, really worried. He needs to know for sure."

"I'm 100 percent certain, as far as my buddy is concerned," answered Sgt. Estes. "Why are you so concerned? It doesn't affect you."

"Maybe not directly. But the ripple effect could be devastating, very devastating!"

"All right. Listen. Tomorrow morning, I will make a call. I will explain what's happening and get you and the mayor some answers. As I've always told you, there is nothing to worry about. Now can we get to bed and get some sleep?"

Even with Sgt. Estes' calming demeanor and words, Jaylyn did not feel reassured. Something just didn't seem right.

CHAPTER 66

The sun had risen on Elwood that Monday morning, just as it had done for the past 140 years. But this was not going to be a typical Monday in Elwood. The events that unfolded would reverberate for years to come.

At nine thirty on that Monday morning, every phone in Buchanan County was abuzz. Social media was exploding. Every news outlet was issuing breaking news headlines and commentary. The unexpected had just happened in the biggest trial in the history of Buchanan County. Most people were in shock. Many were dumbfounded. Some were amazed, confused. No one had seen this coming.

Buchanan County Circuit Court Division 1, 9:00 a.m.

The bailiff announced, "All rise!"

The once-again-packed courtroom stood as Judge Jameson entered.

"You may be seated." Directed Judge Jameson.

After everyone was comfortably seated, he continued, "It has come to the courts understanding that there has been a significant development over the weekend regarding this case. Can someone explain to the court what has transpired?"

Prosecutor Jordan Luzier looked over to the defense table. Defense Attorney Lametrius Brewer stood and spoke.

"Your Honor, it has come to the mutual conclusion and agreement that I can no longer represent this client based upon irreconcilable differences on the direction and/or methods used or needed to be used to offer a comprehensive ethical defense. At this time, Your Honor, I respectfully step down as the representative counsel for Jamal Maxim Brown."

There was a collective gasp. The courtroom then erupted in excited loud chatter. The gavel began pounding furiously on the bench.

"Order! Quiet, please! Order!" shouted Judge Jameson.

The courtroom quieted to a muffled whispering.

"This is your wish, Mr. Brewer?" asked Judge Jameson.

"It is, Your Honor."

"Is this, likewise, the wish of the defendant?" continued Judge Jameson.

Standing, Mayor Brown exclaimed, "It is indeed, Judge!"

"For the court record, please state your name and your relationship to the defendant." Directed Judge Jameson.

"I am Mayor Deiondre Brown, the father of the defendant."

"Is this truly the decision you and your son have mutually reached, free of any coercion, duress, or any other unsavory persuasion?"

"It is, Your Honor."

"The court will duly note that the previously agreed upon contract between the defense attorney, Lametrius Brewer, and the defendant, Jamal Maxim Brown, is hereby severed, dissolute, and void. The court will now ask the prosecuting attorney how they would wish to proceed."

Prosecutor Luzier, looking unfazed by the revelation, responded, "Your Honor, the state wishes to proceed with the case. We would, however, graciously oblige the defendant and his father a brief period of time to enlist the services of another attorney and give that attorney ample time to review evidence and transcript of testimonies up to this point. I do not feel that the state should be penalized because all of a sudden, the defendant and his attorney do not see eye to eye, also considering the state is about to wrap up its side of the argument. Another point, Your Honor, is that it would be unfair to the men and women of this jury, who have sacrificed their valuable time to be responsible civic-minded citizens serving on this panel, to say to them it was all for naught." Prosecutor Luzier sat.

"Thank you, Mr. Luzier. Mr. Brown, how would you like to proceed?"

"Your Honor, I feel we need to start all over. I, we, have to find an attorney, and they need to be able to look over everything. They need to have time to line up witnesses. They need a fresh start. Thank you, sir."

Judge Jameson paused for a brief moment, then spoke, "This trial has been going on for some time now. This jury has indeed put in a lot of time. I do not know, nor care to know, what caused such an abrupt and permanent discourse. Whatever it was is between the parties involved. It, however, will not disrupt the proceedings of this court. Mr. Brown, you and your son will have one week, seven days, to hire another attorney, if that is what you desire. Once hired, that attorney will have ten days to review all the evidence and tran-scripted testimony up to this point. Each step along the way will be reported to and documented by this court. Any deadline missed will result in your forfeiture of extended time as outlined. Understood, Mr. Brown?"

"Yes, sir," answered Mayor Brown.

"This court will stand in recess until nine thirty next Monday morning when we will check on the progress of the defendant and his father's attorney search." The gavel sounded.

"All rise!"

All spectators stood. Once the judge exited the courtroom, there was a mad dash out the doors.

CHAPTER 67

"Some morning, huh?" commented Aunt Alicia.

"I'd say so. Wow!" agreed Bella.

Rey added, "That was from out of nowhere. Did you see how fast everyone got out of that courthouse?"

"I know," said Brayden. "They couldn't wait to call or text somebody. I bet social media is blowing up!"

"What could have caused that?" wondered Bella. "It looked like the mayor and Mr. Brewer were doing just fine with each other."

Aunt Alicia offered, "Well, my guess is that it had something to do with the phone recording. That's just my guess."

Bella was confused. "Why that? They had heard it before, right?"

"It was just something in the way the mayor reacted when Mr. Luzier introduced that piece of evidence…" continued Aunt Alicia.

"You're right," interrupted Brayden. "His attitude just totally changed."

"Yeah, he went from cool and laid back to absolutely frantic," added Rey. "You probably couldn't see that from where you were, Bella."

"No, I didn't see that."

"You know, you're probably right, Aunt Alicia," said Brayden.

"But why?" asked Bella. "It just doesn't make sense."

"True," replied Aunt Alicia. "But we don't know what goes on behind closed doors. We're just left to speculate. It'll all come out eventually. It usually does."

As they sat around eating brunch at Aunt Alicia's, they continued to discuss and question the startling event of that morning. Little did they know, other shocking news was on the way.

CHAPTER 68

"I'm thinking it's time to drop the final shoe," commented PA Jordan Luzier.

"Are all the I's dotted and T's crossed?" queried Assistant Prosecutor Connie Stephens.

"Yes, ma'am. I've checked and rechecked. Everything is ready to go. With what has transpired, I don't think we should hold off any longer."

"Agree. We have to move before they move," affirmed Assistant Stephens.

"Precisely."

PA Luzier picked up the phone, dialed seven digits, then simply said, "It's on." He hung up.

If you thought Monday morning was shocking, just wait until you hear about Monday afternoon.

CHAPTER 69

"Tyler! Get up! You have a visitor!" ordered the jail guard.

"What?" Tyler asked, finding it hard to believe he heard correctly. "Are you sure?"

"I'm sure."

"Who is it?" Tyler continued asking.

The guard answered, "You'll just have to come and see."

"Is it somebody I know?"

"Tyler, quit asking questions. Get up off your butt. Let's go."

Tyler was confused, worried, and excited. He had sat in jail for months and never had one visitor. Not even a phone call. He wondered if it could be the mayor, his son, or a hitman. He didn't know how to feel, happy or scared. He was curious, though. He followed the jail guard to the visitor area.

Seated across from him, on the other side of the glass, was a stunningly beautiful woman. Tyler looked around, as if to indicate this must be some kind of mistake. He looked at her again. She smiled, nodded, and picked up the phone. Tyler did likewise.

"Hi, Tyler," she began. "I came by to let you know your attorney has stepped down."

"What? Why would he do that?" asked a shocked Tyler.

"I don't know. All I know is he will not be representing you any longer."

"Why? When did you find out?"

"Again, I don't know why. I found out today."

"What am I supposed to do? How can that be?"

Tyler continued to try to understand what was happening.

"I don't know what to tell you," she replied.

"Who are you? Who sent you with this crazy news?"

"All I know is your attorney has stepped down. Good luck, Tyler. I wish you the best."

She hung up the phone, stood up, turned, and walked away. Tyler was aghast. He was devastated. He didn't think things could have gotten any worse than they already were. But things had just darkened even more.

Tyler didn't know what to do. He was surely all alone. The only visitor he had had since his incarceration had been his attorney. Now his attorney had stepped down.

Tyler was truly depressed. He felt he no longer had a purpose. He truly felt that his life was over. He wanted to end it all, but he didn't have the strength or the wherewithal.

As he lay in his small jail cell, he kept thinking back on his life with Hailey and Brayden. He had, in his mind, believed he had provided them with a comfortable life. They had money and clothes. They had food and a roof over their heads. What more could they have wanted? Evidently Tyler missed the boat entirely when it came to meaningful relationships and what makes them special.

Suddenly, without warning or prompting, Tyler sprang from the bed and hurried to his cell door. He yelled for a guard. He yelled and yelled.

Finally, a female guard responded, "What you need, Davis?"

"I really need to make a phone call!"

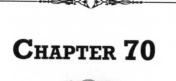

CHAPTER 70

Koen came rushing into his house.

"You have got to turn on the TV! Right now!" he exclaimed.

"Why? What's up?" a confused Jolene asked.

"You have got to see what's happening now in Buchanan County!" explained an excited Koen. "This is unbelievable!"

Jolene quickly turned on the TV. The local four o'clock early edition news was just coming on the air.

NEWS ANCHOR BROOKE MILFELD. In a breaking news report, three very-high-profile Buchanan County residents have been arrested. It comes as a result of an undercover sting operation. We take you live to Anthony Rauls outside the Buchanan County Justice Center.

ANTHONY RAULS, STANDING IN FRONT OF THE JUSTICE CENTER. Good afternoon, Brooke. This has been some day in Buchanan County. First, the proceedings that took place this morning in the high-profile case of the mayor's son, Jamal Brown. Now this. This will surely have people talking.

At about 1:30 p.m. today, the Buchanan County Sheriff's Department and the Kansas State Police executed arrest and search warrants, taking into custody three high-profile Buchanan County officials. Two of the people were Mayor Deiondre Brown and his special assistant, Jaylyn Reese. The other was Sgt. Jase Estes of the Buchanan County Sheriff's Department.

These arrests come as a result of a several-months-long undercover sting conducted jointly by the sheriff's department and the state's attorney general's office.

BROOKE MILFELD. Anthony, is the arrest of Mayor Brown something different from a previous indictment?

ANTHONY. Yes, it is, Brooke. The details and exact charges for this latest incident have not been released as of yet. The Attorney General's Office said they will hold a press conference in a couple of hours where they may be able to provide more details at that time. Reporting live from the Buchanan County Justice Center, I'm Anthony Rauls.

"Wow! What in the world is going on in Buchanan County?" exclaimed Jolene. "Things are getting crazier by the minute!"

CHAPTER 71

Times had been very eventful and exceedingly stressful of late for Mayor Brown. He had been fighting to keep his son out of jail. Plus, due to an earlier indictment, he had been busy trying to figure out how to keep himself free. Now he had another legal predicament to deal with. On top of all that, he has had to hire a new defense attorney for him and his son, Attorney Kenneth "Clyde" Peoples.

If not for Lametrius Brewer, Kenneth Peoples would have been the most-sought-after defense attorney around. He's less extravagant and less flamboyant than Brewer but just as astute and knowledgeable. He's older yet just as sharp. He is straightforward and honest.

Kenneth Peoples said, "This is crazy! How did you expect to get around this?"

Mayor Brown answered, "We thought we had it figured it out, but something went wrong. What do you think?"

"There is no way in hell you get around this!" stated Peoples matter-of-factly. "The prosecution has an open-and-shut case."

"There is nothing?" questioned Mayor Brown. "I mean, there is always a way."

"Mayor, I don't think so. I know you want to protect your son, but there is no way."

"Are you sure? One hundred percent sure?"

"One hundred percent sure. It is irrefutable," stated Peoples.

"Well, what are our options?" inquired Mayor Brown.

"Way I see it," continued Peoples, "you have two viable options. Number one, fight it in court and hope the jury is deaf and blind to the facts, or number two, make a plea deal."

"A plea deal? I don't know. That means admitting guilt," responded Mayor Brown.

"Yes and no," answered Peoples. "You see, we could do an Alford plea. That means we say that there appears to be evidence enough that I might be convicted, but I'm not admitting guilt."

Mayor Brown asked again, "What about a full trial? What do you think?"

"Like I said, the prosecution has an open-and-shut case. I don't think you'll find a blind-enough jury to get him off."

Mayor Brown's world had been turned upside down. His son was facing a felony sexual assault conviction. He himself was facing multiple charges which included felony drug charges, tampering with witnesses, and tampering with evidence. The public was clamoring for his immediate resignation. His name was constantly, consistently in the media spotlight.

Although things and circumstances looked very bleak, Mayor Brown would not concede. He would not accept defeat. He refused to relinquish the hold he has had on power, prestige, and influence.

CHAPTER 72

"You know what would have been awesome?" Bella asked. "If you would have been able to walk with us at graduation."

"Well, I made the mistake, so I had consequences. Life goes on," responded Brayden.

"Understandable, but it would have been great."

"True," answered Brayden. "Don't worry about me not being able to. Think about you doing it. Not just doing it but doing it with honors. That is something to focus on."

Brayden and Bella were at a graduation party hosted by Coach Mac and his wife. It was an elaborate affair. After all, Rey, their only daughter, their only child, had graduated. She was a stellar student, a remarkable athlete, an amazing daughter. Rey had given her adoptive parents the best gift of all—the thrill of parenthood.

They had been scared, frightened. They had doubted their ability to raise a child. Little did they realize they were just like millions and billions of other parents, none know for sure. Just give it your best and pray. That is exactly what the McCullough family did.

"So how are you lovebirds doing?" Rey asked Bella and Brayden.

"We are doing great," answered Bella.

"Hopefully you two are not going to be sitting the whole time you're here. I know you have a lot on your minds, but take some time to just think about nothing. Relax and be a teenager. Mom and Dad feel like we need this."

"They're right," said Brayden. "It's time to enjoy the best of times, the worst of times, better known as the teenage years. We only go through this once. Thank God!"

Rey offered, "There's all kinds of things to do here. So mingle and have fun. Eat, drink, and be merry! This is our time, our day! Enjoy it!"

"C'mon, let's have some fun." Directed Bella.

Brayden and Bella walked off with Rey.

There was plenty to do. They played all the games that were set up. They listened and danced to the music. They took photos. They ate and ate some more. Before they knew it, six hours had passed. Yet they didn't feel like stopping. It felt so good just to be able to relax and forget about the pressures of their worlds, if only for a brief moment.

In two days, all the stress and pressure would be back in full force. Another maddening moment in the growing soap opera of Elwood and Buchanan County.

CHAPTER 73

For the past several days, Jamal has seen his dad as he's never seen him before. Gone was the cockiness, the arrogance, the air of invincibility. Mayor Brown tried to put on a good show in front of his son, but Jamal could tell it was all pretense.

As a result, Jamal seemingly began to sense the beginnings of fallibility in his own armor. He wasn't so confident in his fixer, the one who always made problems disappear. Was this the one thing he wasn't going to be able to make go away? Had the magic run out?

Jamal found himself actually thinking about being convicted. He actually found himself wondering what it would be like to lose his celebrity status in Elwood and Buchanan County.

How could this be? This can't be real! Wait a minute! I'm thinking crazy! Ain't nothing going to change. Dad knows too many people that owe him. All he has to do is pull the right strings, and everything will be back to normal. What was I thinking? Dad's still got it together.

Such were the thoughts of Jamal. Thoughts that he didn't realize were popping in his head several times every day. Maybe he did realize it but refused to acknowledge them as real and concerning.

One thing for sure, he did not realize the strings he figured his dad could pull, well, those strings had been snipped. No longer was there any connection on the other end.

"What did Mr. Peoples say?" asked Jamal.

"Not a whole lot, son," answered Mayor Brown.

"You met with him for quite a long time for him not to say a whole lot."

"Well, Jamal, he didn't say much as far as the options we have at this point."

"What options are there? I'd really like to know what he said."

"As far as he sees it, son, the prosecution has an open-and-shut case. He sees no way around the phone recording. He says if the jury hears that, case closed."

"Do they have to hear it?" Jamal asked.

"I'm afraid so," a worried Mayor Brown answered.

"I don't get it," Jamal responded. "Then what are our options?"

"Well, as Mr. Peoples put it, we can proceed with the trial and hope we have a deaf, blind, and dumb jury, and they acquit. That chance is slim to none. The other choice is to work out a plea deal—"

"I'm not pleading guilty to nothing! That is not an option!" Jamal exploded. He was not going to say he was guilty of anything.

He had never had to admit to any wrongdoing his whole life. Why should he be expected to do so now?

CHAPTER 74

Monday Morning, 7:45 a.m.

Attorney Kenneth Peoples was already in his office. He was preparing to meet with Mayor Deiondre Brown and Jamal. Today court would reconvene for Jamal's case, and Mr. Peoples wanted to make sure he and the Browns were on the same page regarding how to proceed. After having had explained and discussed the possible options, Mr. Peoples was fairly certain he understood which route the Browns wanted to take, but he knew people had a tendency to change their minds. Thus he wanted to be certain before they walked into the courtroom.

Eight o'clock came and went, as did 8:15 a.m. Peoples knew that Mayor Brown was not one to be late. He began to wonder if something had come up to delay them. At 8:30 a.m., Peoples was really worried.

"Mrs. Jackson." Peoples called to his secretary, "You did call the Browns, right?"

"Yes, I did," she replied. "No one answered so I left a voice mail message."

"What time was that?"

"Around 8:20 a.m."

"Hmmm. Something doesn't seem right. Try them one more time. Let me know what you get."

"Sure thing, Mr. Peoples."

Mrs. Jackson made the call. It went directly to voice mail. She left another message. When she informed Peoples that there was still no answer, she could see the look of consternation on his face.

Something was not right. Something was terribly wrong.

CHAPTER 75

It had been a couple weeks since Lametrius Brewer had stepped down as the lead counsel for Jamal and Mayor Brown. He was in unfamiliar territory. He had always been the one in the spotlight. Now he was not. He had always been the one spending countless hours in his office in preparation. Now he was not.

He had completely cleared his calendar and had not taken on any new clients so he could devote all his attention to the Browns' cases. He now actually had nothing to do. Yet he didn't mind it at all.

"What do you plan to do with all your free time?" Koen inquired of his father.

"Good question. But I'm not even worried about it. It actually feels pretty good," answered Brewer.

"What about your clients?"

"Well, as of right now, I don't have any clients, and I don't know if I'll go looking anytime soon for any new ones."

Koen was surprised to hear that come out of his father's mouth.

"Am I hearing you right? That doesn't sound like the Lametrius Brewer I know."

"I know. I shocked myself. I don't think I have ever experienced true downtime. I don't think I ever let myself stop working. I've always been too caught up in being on top, on being the best. I've always been 24-7, 365. Never had time to stop and smell the roses. But now that I've had this break, I'm loving it. It's exactly what I've needed."

"I like what I'm hearing, Dad. There really are a lot of wonderful things in this world. We just have to take the time to go out and enjoy them."

Lametrius Brewer was looking at things from a different perspective. He was no longer trying to poke holes in the prosecution's case, no longer trying to create reasonable doubt.

"Dad, I'm very proud of you," said Koen.

"Thanks, son. Right is right."

"Since when has that been your philosophy?"

"I've always believed that. It's just in the line of a defense attorney, people think you don't care what is right. They think you want to circumvent justice. The thing is, it's up to the prosecution to seal the deal. If they left me an opening, I pounced, and I pounced hard. I did what the system allowed me to do, simple as that. Did some people who should have been locked up get away? Certainly. Reasonable doubt. No one got off because I lied or cheated."

"But, Dad, it always appeared like you enjoyed what you were doing."

"Oh, I enjoyed the game, the chess match. I didn't necessarily enjoy defending the guilty, but according to our system, they deserve proper and adequate representation. I always made sure I gave them just that. Plus the guilty pay well, very well."

"So it was mainly the money," Koen said. "That's what you were in it for."

"Not quite. As I said, I loved the game, the challenge. The money made life easier. I will admit, that is what attracted me to the defense side to begin with. Then my ego took over."

Ego can be a powerful and dangerous shaper of self-worth, self-esteem, self-identity, and self-importance. Often people are told to keep their ego in check. Some do. Some don't.

CHAPTER 76

Monday at 9:30 a.m.

"Your Honor, I am at a loss," began Mr. Peoples. "We were to meet at eight o'clock this morning to discuss today's proceedings. My clients never showed."

"Was there any attempt made to contact your clients?" inquired Judge Jameson.

"Yes, sir. Several attempts. Around 8:45 a.m., my office even contacted the Buchanan County Sheriff's Department asking them to do a welfare check. As of this moment, I have not heard anything from the Sheriff's Department."

"Mr. Luzier, how does the state wish to proceed?" asked Judge Jameson.

"Your Honor, the state is willing to agree to a short recess, if the court wishes to grant such, to allow Mr. Peoples the opportunity to find out what the welfare check uncovered."

In agreement, Judge Jameson directed. "A short recess shall be granted. The court will reconvene at 11:00 a.m."

The gavel sounded.

After the courtroom cleared, Prosecutor Luzier and Attorney Peoples turned and looked at each other.

Peoples shrugged and said, "This is crazy weird. I never thought something like this would happen."

Luzier countered. "Don't feel like the Lone Ranger. Nobody saw this coming."

CHAPTER 77

"This court stuff is not making sense," said a confused Bella.

"I don't get what's going on either," replied Rey.

"I can't believe they didn't show up this morning." Chimed in Aunt Alicia. "That is not like the Browns. They always show up to be the center of attention. Something's weird."

Bella wondered, "Do you think something happened to them?"

"Hard to say," answered Aunt Alicia.

"We should find out soon," added Rey. "By the way, where is Brayden this morning?"

"He had to meet with the assistant prosecutor," informed Bella. "There was something that came up over the weekend, and they needed to see him immediately this morning."

"Interesting," said Rey.

"Hey, we've got a little more than an hour before we have to be back here in court. Let's go to that new donut shop down the block and get some unhealthy food and drink," suggested Aunt Alicia.

Bella and Rey were in total agreement. So off they went, wondering what strange happening was going to occur next.

CHAPTER 78

Earlier Monday Morning

Brayden had been summoned to meet with Assistant Prosecutor Connie Stephens.

"What's going on?" asked Brayden. "Does it have to do with my case?"

"No, Brayden. You are fine," said Ms. Stephens.

"Whew, I was pretty worried. I thought I had done something to revoke my SMART program status."

"Not at all, but we had a surprising development over the weekend. Something we felt you should know about."

Brayden immediately became worried. "Is my mom all right?"

"She's fine. She's in good hands," said Ms. Stephens. "It's your dad."

Brayden leaned back in the chair. He hadn't seen his dad nor had he talked to him since he had been kicked out of the house months ago. Brayden still harbored a very strong dislike for him. Yet he couldn't help but feel concern and wonder if something bad had happened to him.

"Did somebody finally get to him and bust his head open?" asked Brayden, trying not to sound too caring.

"No, he's safe," said Ms. Stephens.

"Well, what did he do then?"

"Well, believe it or not, Brayden, your dad has had a change of heart."

Brayden was unsure what Ms. Stephens meant by that. "How you figure that?"

"He made a frantic call to our office. He wants to tell us everything he knows. Why he all of a sudden decided to do this, we really don't know. We have no idea. But if he's sincere, he could really slam some doors shut on a lot of people."

"I don't get that," said Brayden. "He's always been so loyal to his people. He was more protective of them than he was of his own family. Strange."

"You know, Brayden, he has been locked up for months, basically all alone with nothing to do but think. He really had no visitors. His attorney abandoned him. Maybe he figured that instead of just rotting in a jail cell by himself, he wanted to make sure some other individuals got what they deserved."

"I don't know," wondered Brayden. "He's never been one to rat anybody out. He's never had the balls to do that. Excuse my language."

"No problem. I've heard worse," said Ms. Stephens. "Jail can change a person, you know. There are actually some people that do get rehabilitated. Maybe your dad is one of them."

"We'll see," said an unconvinced Brayden. "All this being said, why was it so important for me to be here this morning?"

CHAPTER 79

Monday, 11:00 a.m.

The bailiff announced, "All rise!"

Judge Jameson entered, sat, and directed the packed courtroom. "Please be seated."

He continued, "Before we bring the jury in, we are going to figure out if we are actually ready to proceed with the case. As I look at the defense table, I do not see the defendant in this matter. Mr. Peoples, could you please inform the court as to what information you were able to ascertain from the previously mentioned welfare check conducted by the Buchanan County Sheriff's Department?"

Mr. Peoples stood and said, "Your Honor, the welfare check came up empty. No contact was made with the defendant or his father. The Sheriff's Department did say there were no immediate signs of any measures of foul play at the residence. As of this moment, they have not been located. Also my office has repeatedly called all known phone numbers of my clients, and all we get is voice mail. We've even reached out to anyone we thought might have seen or heard from them in the last few days. To no avail."

"Today was the day we were to reconvene this case," said Judge Jameson. "It had been on hold for a couple of weeks. It was time to resume. However, it is obvious right now that we cannot. Also it is obvious that the defendant has skipped out on his obligation to appear in court at the scheduled appointed time. It is, therefore, the duty of this court to issue a warrant for the immediate arrest of Jamal Maxim Brown as a fugitive of justice. The state is ordered to execute said warrant and bring said subject in front of this court to answer to all charges. The present case shall be suspended indefinitely. The jury shall be instructed accordingly. This court is adjourned."

The gavel sounded. Another unexpected development. Was Jamal really a fugitive of justice or was something more sinister at play?

CHAPTER 80

Anna Maria Island has always been a favorite spot for tourists. But it doesn't have that typical tourist atmosphere. It has a feel of small-town America, from its quaint shops like Ginny's and Jane E's to The Sandbar Restaurant to The Rod and Reel Pier. It's a place where a person can actually sit, observe, and truly relax and detach completely from the regular stressors of one's life, whether it be at the public beach or at a private beach.

A middle-aged man sat on a second-story balcony of a condo overlooking a private beach. He observed below him the activities on the beach—walking, running, sunning, relaxing, etc. There was activity in the water as well—swimming, boating, parasailing, Jet Skiing, etc. Families and individuals were walking to and from the beach. There was fun, excitement, and enjoyment.

The middle-aged man then looked out at the vastness of the gulf waters. The distant waters had a look of quiet and smoothness, as slick as glass. But as he looked to the waters closer to shore, they were choppier and rougher. He compared the sights to his life. From a distance, everything looked smooth and quiet. But the closer one got, the more unsettled everything was. As a matter of fact, the closer you got, the more it looked like hurricane conditions.

The middle-aged man knew that this visit to Anna Maria Island was only for a short stop off. He wasn't going to have time to truly take it all in, soak it up, and enjoy it fully. His tumultuous life circumstances demanded he move on and move on quickly. Cuba was calling. Cuba was yelling. And Mayor Deiondre Brown was listening.

What was he doing on Anna Maria Island? Wasn't he supposed to be in Elwood in Buchanan County? Wasn't he supposed to be supporting his son in the darkest hour of his son's young life? Come to think of it, where was his son? Where was Jamal?

He was right where he had always been throughout his entire life—under his father's protective wing.

The Browns were on the lam.

CHAPTER 81

The Buchanan County Sheriff's Department Fugitive Squad applied for and was granted a search warrant for the Brown residence. They had their work cut out for them.

The Brown home was palatial. Located just outside the city limits, the twelve-thousand-square-foot home sat on fifteen acres of plush land. Other than the pool house, there were no outbuildings to speak of, no toolsheds, no detached garages. Because of the vastness of the area to be searched, the detectives knew they had many long arduous hours ahead of them. They were looking for any sign of foul play or anything that might lead to the whereabouts of the Browns.

One of the first things noticed was an empty space in the five-car garage. Having checked on the vehicles registered to the Browns, one was missing a 2018 BMW X5 SUV, black in color. Immediately a BOLO (be on the lookout) was issued for the vehicle, locally and to surrounding jurisdictions.

There was security surveillance on the property, but it appears to have been disabled. That in itself was strange. Why would it be disabled? When was it disabled? It wasn't like Mayor Brown to have his property unprotected, unsecured.

The worry of the investigators heightened. It wasn't so much a concern about the safety or welfare of the Browns. The missing car, the disconnected security system, no visible signs of forced entry, no signs of struggle or theft, all this led the investigators to believe one thing—the Browns were fleeing. The worry was how much of a head start they had. The questions they had were: When did they leave? What direction did they go? What was the planned final destination? Did they have help?

Immediately an investigation was begun into the Browns' financial accounts in an attempt to track movement. It was discovered that large amounts of cash were withdrawn from several of the six accounts they held. These transactions occurred on the preceding Friday. The total sum came to $40,000.

The investigators knew they were behind the eight ball. They also knew that a lot of affluent people who go on the run most likely try to get to a place that does not have an extradition treaty with the United States. Forty grand could get someone a long way in a short period of time.

Where would they go? Were they there already? What, or who, can lead us to them?

Only time would tell. And time was of the essence.

CHAPTER 82

"Has anyone interviewed Reese or Estes yet?" asked Lt. Marcus Riney.

Lt. Riney was in the office of Prosecuting Attorney Luzier. They were discussing the proceedings of Monday morning. They were surprised yet not totally.

"You know Reese organized everything for Mayor Brown," continued Lt. Riney.

"So true," answered PA Luzier. "You don't think they have flown the coop too, do you?"

"I don't think so. Estes is not a runner. He'll face the music. Although to be honest, I've never known him to be in trouble, especially this magnitude of trouble."

"I will be sending a couple of my investigators to talk to them. Think they'll say anything?" asked PA Luzier.

"I truly doubt it. But you never know. Stranger things have happened. Although can't possibly be much stranger than what's already happened."

CHAPTER 83

"It's a pleasure to finally meet you," said Lametrius Brewer to his new daughter-in-law, Jolene.

Jolene responded, "Likewise. I've heard a lot about you."

"I bet you have. Despite what you've heard, I'm not all bad. I've had some issues, but I guess that goes with the territory of a driven personality."

"Believe it or not," began Jolene, "It wasn't all bad. Besides, I tend to look for the good in almost everything, everyone, and every situation."

"Almost to a fault." Chimed in Koen.

"I know. I know. I'm working on it," confessed Jolene.

"We've all got our issues, that's for sure," affirmed Brewer. "At least, other than Koen. He seems to have it all together."

"Ha ha. Very funny, Dad," retorted Koen. "We don't have time to go through all my issues."

Brewer was enjoying spending time with Koen, just getting the opportunity to hold a normal, decent, constructive conversation. There were times when he thought he had totally destroyed the chance to build a relationship with his son. He knew it would take some time, now that he was given the opportunity. He was willing to do whatever it took.

"Dad, I really appreciate you coming by our humble abode and having dinner."

"Hey, son, the invitation is greatly appreciated."

"Speaking of dinner," Jolene interceded, "It is served. Come help yourself."

The mood was light, happy, and very relaxing. The meal prepared by Jolene was excellent. Everything was going great.

"Can I get a little personal and nosy with you two?" asked Brewer.

Koen, as he gave Jolene a quizzical uneasy glance, responded, "Well, I don't know. Depends on what you're getting into."

"You know you can always tell me to mind my own business," said Brewer. "I was just wanting to ask you about your living conditions. You know, your housing, are you buying, renting, or what?"

"Okay. So why do you want to know that?" inquired Koen. "Are you about to give us a lesson on how wrong we are in what we are doing?"

Koen was starting to think, *Here we go. Same old Dad. Can't get beyond critiquing everybody. Doesn't think I'm adult enough.*

Brewer laughed and said, "Oh, no. Not at all. I understand your skepticism. After all, that's all you've ever known me to do. This is different."

"How so?" Koen wanted to know.

"Well, I know sometimes it can be a little tough for young couples getting started, especially housing. So I want to help you out. If you will let me."

"In what way?" asked Koen.

Brewer began explaining, "I've got this place on the west side that is actually relatively new, maybe five years old at most. It has four bedrooms, three and a half baths, fully furnished basement, three-car attached garage, a huge backyard, a patio and deck. However, it doesn't have a pool."

"How horrible!" exclaimed Koen sarcastically. "That's an amazing-sounding place, Dad. Are you needing someone to lease it? Are you wanting us to? What would be the terms?"

"No, no. Nothing like that. I don't want you to rent or lease or buy. I want to give it to you."

Koen and Jolene sat there wide-eyed, open-mouthed.

Brewer continued, "You can think about it. I just thought it might help you out a little. I'm not trying to buy back a relationship. It's just that if I've got something, and I'm not using it, I might as well give it to someone who can. True? Plus who knows, maybe you'll be thinking about expanding the family soon. You'll already have plenty of room and no mortgage payment."

"Dad...I...I just don't know what...what to say." Stammered Koen. "This is totally unexpected."

"That's an amazing offer, Mr. Brewer," added Jolene.

"One, it's not an offer, it's a gift," corrected Brewer. "And two, do not call me Mr. Brewer. It's Lametrius or, even better, Dad."

Koen and Jolene didn't know what to do or say. They were astonished.

"Oh yeah, and another thing." Brewer went on. "I know this will knock you dead."

"I'm already knocked dead," Koen managed to utter.

"Well, this is gonna knock you deader. I called your mom."

Koen was floored!

CHAPTER 84

Brayden and Bella were sitting on a park bench along the lake in Elwood City Park. Though it was warm, it was relaxing, peaceful, and breezy. They were thinking back on and talking about the events that have occurred in their lives just in the past year. It was hard for them to fathom that so much had happened and that they were smack-dab in the middle of it all. Through the turmoil and confusion, they were fortunate enough to have found each other. They were able to become each other's rock and shoulder to lean on.

They also realized things were not yet over.

Bella had no idea when the trial would resume, and Brayden had no idea when his trials would begin. Every day there seemed to be some sort of new twist or turn or strange occurrence happening.

Brayden's dad had decided to turn state's evidence, become a state witness. Such would probably alleviate any need for Brayden or his mother, Hailey, having to testify.

Bella had heard that the Browns could not be found. She didn't know if that was a good thing or a bad thing. All she knew was that it would prolong her stress related to the trial. She was ready for it to be over. College was right around the corner. She didn't want to have any distractions going into her freshman year.

Brayden was constantly worried about his mother. He hadn't seen her in months, ever since she was put in protective custody. He couldn't see her or talk to her. He wasn't allowed to know where she was. He would only get periodic reports from the prosecutor's office telling him his mother was doing fine. He wanted more. He needed more.

Such were the lives of these two. They understood the principle that growth creates change, and change can cause stress. They just weren't counting on so much stress and change all at one time.

CHAPTER 85

Wednesday Morning

"When do we get out of here? It's already been three days!" Jamal complained.

He and his father were still on Anna Marie Island having breakfast at Ginny's and Jane E's Café and Gift Store. They were trying to enjoy an order of two Ginny Skillets, fresh fruit, a latte, and a Monkey Business smoothie. They even ordered one of the restaurant's signature cinnamon buns.

Mayor Brown was trying to maintain an inconspicuous presence, though he himself was starting to become anxious.

"I know. These things take time," answered Mayor Brown.

Jamal was unsatisfied.

"I thought you said we had to move quickly. This doesn't seem like it to me."

"Well, if all we had to do was hop on a commercial flight or ship, it would be quick and simple. But we have to be very discreet. Unfortunately we have to bide our time until others get things situated."

"That's crazy! That's freakin' ridiculous!" Jamal continued to complain.

"Maybe so. Due to the nature of our journey, the type of transportation we need is not easy to set up. So try to relax and be patient, and try not to draw attention to us," cautioned Mayor Brown. "We should be hearing something within the next day or so."

A short distance across the room, a family of four was finishing up their morning meal and preparing to head out to a day at the beach. The father softly nudged his wife and whispered, "Isn't that Jamal Brown and his dad?"

CHAPTER 86

Wednesday Afternoon

"It's my understanding that your husband, Tyler, wants to turn state's evidence," said Detective Samantha Pope (Sam).

"Oh, really. I never would have thought that," replied Hailey. "He was always so loyal to his partners. I wonder what changed his mind."

"Well," began Sam, "I think one reason was because he was left fending for himself, all by himself. His attorney left him. No one visited him. He was literally all alone. He may have begun to really fear for his safety."

"That's sad. But people will do you that way. When things are going smoothly, you are okay. Soon as the wagon turns, they abandon you."

"That's for sure," agreed Sam.

A sincerely concerned Hailey asked, "How is he doing?"

"To be truthful," said Sam, "he's a total mess. His mental stability is shot. Physically, not very fit. Though he never was very stout, now he's quite frail. Jail has not been good to him."

Hailey, with a look of sadness, said, "Sorry to hear that."

Sam, noticing the unhappy look on Hailey's face, asked, "Does that bother you?"

"It bothers me some. I mean, we were together for more than half my life. I care about him and hope he stays well. I don't hate the man. I just know he's going to need help. Probably lots of it."

"You're probably right, Hailey."

CHAPTER 87

"I totally misjudged you. I never thought you would do this to me. You absolutely stabbed me in the back!"

Such began the conversation between Sgt. Jase Estes and Lt. Marcus Riney.

The two were meeting in the deposition room of the prosecutor's office. Sgt. Estes had called Prosecutor Luzier and requested the meeting with Lt. Riney. This was the first time they had seen each other since Sgt. Estes was arrested. Needless to say, Sgt. Estes was upset.

It stemmed from the fact that Sgt. Estes tried to get Lt. Riney involved in some unscrupulous activity. Estes wanted Riney to be a part of the plan to tamper with some very incriminating and damning evidence against Jamal Brown, namely the phone recording of the incident involving Bella Seger. Estes thought he had Riney in his pocket, just because of their close personal friendship. Riney, instead, sank deeper into his undercover persona.

"I'm sorry you feel that way, Jase," replied Lt. Riney.

"How else would I feel? You ratted me out!"

"So that's really how you see it?"

"You better believe it!" said a visibly agitated Sgt. Estes. "We were supposed to be friends! We were supposed to be tight!"

Lt. Riney shook his head, leaned back in his chair, and calmly stated, "Look, when I began my career, who was my training officer? Who was the guy I spent every day of my first three months on the road with? Who taught me the ins and outs of police work? Can you answer me that?"

Sgt. Estes did not respond, so Lt. Riney continued, "By the way, who was the one guy who kept drilling into my head that honesty and integrity were the most important qualities of a good police officer? Who told me, 'Never bend the rules. More importantly, never break the rules'? Who was that guy? We both know who that was. It was the same guy who, at one time, believed upholding the law was one of the noblest things a person could do. It was the same guy who built a career on trust. The same guy who the public revered. It's the same guy who is sitting across from me right now. The same guy who is having a hard time owning up to his transgression."

Lt. Riney paused, then said, "I don't know what happened to you in the last year or so. All I know is you are a changed man." Then he added, "Speaking of misjudging someone, looks like I was totally wrong about you."

Sgt. Estes continued to sit silently. He didn't look up at Lt. Riney. He sat with his hands interlocked on the table. He stared down at his hands.

Lt. Riney studied him. He knew Sgt. Estes was upset, but he knew it was directed inwardly. A fall from grace is never easy to accept or deal with.

"Well, since you have nothing to say, I'm leaving. I've got things to do. I'm assuming all you wanted to do was chew me out for doing my job. I think you got your chance for that."

Lt. Riney stood up and said, "Good luck to you, Jase."

As he was turning to walk away, Sgt. Estes quietly said, "Wait a minute."

CHAPTER 88

Thursday, a.m.

"Ms. Reese, thanks for wanting to talk to us," acknowledged Assistant Prosecutor Connie Stephens.

Jaylyn Reese had always been someone who seemed to have always had everything together, even as a young girl.

She was the youngest of three children being raised by a single mother. Her mother and father divorced when she was four years old. Her father was not one who regularly paid his obligated child support. As a matter of fact, he made a grand total of five payments. Then he disappeared, not wanting to have anything to do with the children.

Jaylyn's mother, needless to say, struggled to provide for the children. She took odd jobs and did the best she could. At one point in time, she had to revert to the oldest profession known to man. It was nothing she was proud of, and it was something she desperately tried to hide from her children. At the time, she felt it was her only choice. She knew she had to feed, clothe, and house her children.

Jaylyn always seemed to look past the family's low-class economic status. She always had visions of grandeur. She truly loved all the glitz and glamour she saw on TV and in the movies. She dreamed of a life of luxury. She dreamed of a life of privilege.

At an early age, she learned how to manipulate, influence, and get her way. She became very adept at using her good looks and charm to lift her status and influence among her peers. Through junior high and high school, she commanded the attention of the most affluent, athletic, and popular male students. They showered her with gifts, including cash money.

Jaylyn also learned to mask darkness. To her, her darkness was defined in her family's lack of wealth. Unable to afford the finer things, Jaylyn figured out how to make the cheap hand-me-down items look great. She would never bring friends to her family house, although their modest home was always clean and well kept. Her mother was always working, so that fueled her excuses for not having company over, especially boys.

Upon graduation, Jaylyn decided not pursue college life. She was able to land jobs working in various offices around town. The majority of the offices were those of the most prestigious individuals and/or businesses. It was not necessarily her credentials that landed her those positions, but more so her great looks. However, to her credit, she learned her jobs and did them well. She regularly garnered promotions, the majority of which were warranted. Her last promotion, three years ago, was that of special assistant to the mayor.

CHAPTER 89

Betrayal has been documented throughout history. From the Garden of Eden to Samson and Delilah, from Brutus to Judas to Benedict Arnold, from Dona Marina to Julius and Ethel Rosenberg and countless others.

How many of us have been betrayed in some way or another? What brings about betrayal? How does one get to that point?

First, a relationship has to develop between consenting parties. Over time that relationship intensifies. It grows and becomes stronger. A true bond develops. An overwhelming trust and confidence blossoms. Secrets and emotions are shared. Comfort is experienced.

Suddenly one party decides to destroy that seemingly indestructible camaraderie. They belie the trust and confidence. But why?

Most often it is for personal gain. They look to receive some sort of compensation, be it monetary, favor, privilege, or leniency. They feel they can better their own lot by damaging the lot of someone else.

Even those dealing in dirt can be betrayed. Their partners in crime turn on them, usually upon facing big trouble. Loyalty goes out the window. It becomes a me thing. What can I do for *me*? How can I help *me*?

The air of Buchanan County was saturated with betrayal. So many were looking for a deal. They sought to minimize their own indiscretion by any means. They didn't care what they had to do.

CHAPTER 90

Saturday, 3:00 a.m.

"There's a light on and movement," came the first transmission.

"They're just now arriving at the dock," was the second transmission.

*****

Mayor Deiondre Brown's cellphone rang. "Hello," he said.

"Your ride is here," was the response on the other end.

As he hung up, Mayor Brown said, "Time to go."

"It's about time!" answered Jamal. "Let's get out of here!"

"I'm with you, son. Grab your bag and come on."

Mayor Brown and Jamal picked up their respective duffel bags and walked out the front door. They were all smiles as they made their way to the awaiting Cadillac Escalade. They knew they were just moments away from "freedom," as they called it. Just get on a boat and sail off into the vast gulf waters and head toward Havana.

"Let's get movin', Mr. Brown," said the man opening the back of the vehicle so they could deposit their bags.

He was a big man. Over six feet tall. Muscular build. The driver was even bigger. They were in a hurry. Mayor Brown and Jamal threw their bags into the back. They then got into the back seat area of the Escalade, and the vehicle pulled off with the two huge men in the front seats.

"They're off," came the radio transmission.

The Escalade pulled out of the condo complex and headed south on Gulf Drive.

Seconds later, another radio transmission. "They just passed marker *A*."

"Let's do this!" Came the radio response.

In an instant, police vehicles—marked and unmarked—surrounded the Escalade and initiated a felony car stop. There were lots of flashing red and blue lights.

The occupants of the Escalade were caught totally off guard. Several assault rifles, as well as shotguns, were aimed at the vehicle. There was nowhere to go. An attempt to flee would be futile as well as deadly. The four just sat frozen for about thirty seconds. Then as commanded, the driver slowly opened the door and slowly exited the vehicle with his hands in clear view.

"Interlock your fingers and place your hands on top of your head." Pause. "Now slowly walk backward until I tell you to stop," continued the commands. The driver did as told and was taken into custody.

The process was repeated for the three other occupants of the Escalade. All were taken into custody without incident. The four were transported to the Sarasota County Jail for processing.

What the Browns thought was going to be their ticket to escape turned out to be a one-way ticket to incarceration.

At the same time the vehicle stop was being carried out, the US Coast Guard was boarding a boat that had pulled into the Bradenton Beach Marina. Aboard were two men and one woman. They too were taken into custody without incident and taken to the Manatee County Jail.

After the boat was secured and inventoried, several peculiar things were observed: ten large suitcases that appeared fully packed, five passports lying out on a cabin bed, two male wigs, several fake mustaches/beards. To the authorities, it looked like escape paraphernalia.

CHAPTER 91

That same Saturday morning, around 4:30 a.m., a phone rang in the office of PA Luzier. One would have thought it would have just rung and rung until voice mail picked up. But that Saturday morning, the office was filled with anxious individuals. It was reminiscent of the situation room in the White House when US Special Forces took down Osama bin Laden.

The room had been packed since 1:30 a.m. Present was PA Luzier, Lt. Marcus Riney, US Marshall service regional agent-in-charge, FBI regional agent-in-charge, Buchanan County sheriff Jerry Mandela, Assistant PA Connie Stephens, plus a couple of investigators of the prosecutor's office and Elwood chief of police Kelly Jordan. When the phone rang, there was immediate silence, and it seemed like everyone immediately held their breath.

The regional agent-in-charge of the FBI took the call. He listened for a few seconds, nodded his head a couple of times, turned to the crowd in the room. "Seven in custody, including the Browns. No incidents."

Elation and high-fives filled the room. A successful coordinated effort.

By the time noon rolled around, everybody in Buchanan County had heard the news. Many were surprised the Browns had been caught. Most figured they were too connected and could end up anywhere in the world in a moment's notice.

One person who believed that was Tyler Davis. He always felt Mayor Brown was the most connected, most influential, most dangerous man in the world. Tyler believed from the very beginning of all this mess, that he and he alone would be the only one to take the fall. Everybody else, he thought, was too high up to be messed with. He's beginning to see such was not the case.

CHAPTER 92

"Well, well," said Lametrius Brewer, glancing up at a wall-mounted TV in the dining area of Mama Lucia's.

"What's that?" asked Kaneisha Edwards, Koen's mother, Brewer's ex.

"The Browns are no longer on the run. They've been apprehended down in Florida. Early this morning. How about that?"

"Why are you smiling so big?"

"Well, they deserved to get caught. Plus, Mayor Brown seemed to always think he was the sharpest knife in the drawer and could outwit anybody. He always felt he was going to get his way, whatever he wanted."

"Sounds like someone else we both know."

"Hey, hey! Be nice now. I know I got caught up in power, influence, and luxury," confessed Brewer. "I know it's hard to believe, but I've grown up and changed. I'm looking at life through different lenses now."

Kaneisha questioned, "What brought about this drastic transformation? And how do you know it's not for just a short time, and in six months or less, you'll be right back to the same old Lametrius everyone has known for the past twenty-five, thirty years? Change is hard, and it usually doesn't happen overnight."

"First of all, dealing with the egotistical, narcissistic, unethical Deiondre Brown forced me to take a look at myself. I hadn't done that in many, many years. And what I saw, I really didn't like. Matter of fact, I hated what I saw. I looked back on what I was willing to compromise to get a victory. Sure I gained a reputation but at the cost of integrity, fairness, honesty, trustworthiness. It should have been the other way around. I can't do it anymore. I won't do it anymore!

"As I reflected, the thing that got to me the most was truly understanding how much I had hurt the two people who truly loved me and that I truly love. To haunt me the rest of my days will be the thought of all the good times I missed out on and ruined. But I am able to apologize, say I am sorry. I've wronged some very special people. I've got a lot of groveling to do, but I'm willing to do it. I'm not going into it expecting to be forgiven. That doesn't matter. It's just something that has to be done."

For the first time in many years, Lametrius Brewer and Kaneisha Edwards were sitting at the same table in the same eating establishment. Not only that, they were also having what appeared to be a very civil conversation.

When Brewer had told Koen that he had called his mother, Koen was not very sure she would want to waste time talking to his dad. Brewer was, most likely, very persistent, and Koen was secretly hoping they would at least make time to talk and clean up some of the dirty air between them.

Brewer, with a lot of help from Koen, was wholeheartedly trying to become a changed man, trying to make amends, trying to right some wrongs, trying to create a new path. Koen could sense the sincerity and was pulling for him.

Having heard that his parents were going to meet for lunch, Koen could only cross his fingers and pray.

CHAPTER 93

"What a weekend, Aunt Alicia," commented Bella. "I'm so relieved they caught them."

"You and me both, dear. I still can't believe they ran. I always felt they were too arrogant to run. Too confident," said Aunt Alicia.

"I think their apple cart got upset," replied Bella. "It seems they knew that recording was their undoing because a lot changed after that."

Aunt Alicia agreed, "You're right. They really got weird after that was introduced."

"What's next?"

"Good question," answered Aunt Alicia. "I'm sure Mr. Luzier will contact us pretty soon and let us know what the next step is."

"I just want to get this over with," confessed Bella.

"I know. I know. We all do. Believe me, we all do."

There was a knock at the front door. Aunt Alicia opened it, and there stood a visibly upset Rey.

"Honey, what's wrong?" asked a caring, worried Aunt Alicia.

Just when there appeared to be peace and normalcy on the horizon, another cloud appeared.

"You talked to Coach?" asked Bella.

"Yes, I did," answered Rey, "and it didn't go so well. You know he's from way back in his thinking."

"Sorry to hear that," Bella responded.

"I don't want to pry," interjected Aunt Alicia, "but what might y'all be talking about?"

Bella looked at Rey. Rey looked at Bella. Rey looked down at the table.

"Sorry," said Aunt Alicia. "That's okay. You don't have to say anything. I was being nosy. Forgive me."

"No, no," disagreed Rey. "It's okay. I don't mind letting you in on anything. You're like a second mom to me. I probably should have told you earlier. I just didn't want things said before I could talk to my dad."

"You're not pregnant, are you?" questioned Aunt Alicia.

"No, not at all," answered Rey. "I'm gay."

To Aunt Alicia's lack of amazement, Rey said, "You took that pretty well. That didn't shock you?"

"Not at all. It's not like I expected it, but I'm not shocked. If that makes any sense."

"It does. When I told Mom, she didn't know how to react at first. It took a little bit, but she has come to accept it. Dad not so much."

"So Coach didn't take it well," said Bella.

"No," said Rey. "He's so old school. He just stomped around, mumbling to himself. He wasn't mad, but you could tell he wasn't happy. He just walked out of the room and hasn't talked to me in a couple days. Mom says give him some time."

"I'm sure he understands that that sort of lifestyle is really common now, and people don't hide it anymore," commented Bella.

"Yeah, but not his girl. Not his daughter. That's not the way he envisioned things."

Aunt Alicia asked, "Well, how did he envision things?"

"Well, I am his only child. His only daughter. He always dreamed of me growing up, getting married, and having his grandchildren. I think he thinks that is all down the drain now."

"That's all still possible. Every bit of it," argued Bella.

"I know," said Rey. "I'll give him some time. I'll be leaving for college in a few weeks and will be pretty busy for a while. That'll give him some space. I just don't want him to disown me."

"I don't think that will happen," assured Aunt Alicia. "There's too much love there. Time will be a big help."

"Plus I know he'll want to come see you play," added Bella. "He's not going to miss that."

"I hope you're right. I just felt I had to come clean and let them know. Now I wonder if I did the right thing."

"You did the right thing. You had to be true to yourself. You had to release that pent-up reality. You don't have to hide anymore. You can finally be the real you," counseled Bella.

"You sound like some sophisticated therapist," marveled Rey.

"I tell you. She's pretty sharp," commented Aunt Alicia.

Rey felt better about her revelation to her dad after talking to Bella and Aunt Alicia. She felt she had done the right thing, but like us all, she needed some affirmation. She got it, and now she felt better about trying to move on.

The truth shall set you free.

CHAPTER 94

"So, Mr. Brown," Defense Attorney Peoples began. "Things have become a great deal more complicated."

"I understand that," replied a contrite Mayor Brown.

"How do you wish to proceed?" asked Peoples.

Mayor Brown was never one to back down or feel that he was defeated. He always had something up his sleeve. But now, even he realized there was not anything he could do. He was caught. Backed into a corner. Trying to flee was an implication that he was guilty of all the other charges previously filed against him. He couldn't get out of this. You can believe he tried to think of something, but he couldn't.

"What are all the charges against me?" inquired Mayor Brown.

Peoples answered, "Well, let's see. There's fleeing to avoid prosecution, aiding and abetting, reference taking your son away from his trial, racketeering, money laundering, tampering with evidence—"

"Okay, okay," interrupted Mayor Brown. "It certainly doesn't look good, does it? How should I proceed?"

"That's my question to you. How do you want to go forward? We can still go to trial and put your fate in the hands of a jury, or we can try to work out some kind of plea deal. It's your call."

Mayor Brown pondered and then asked, "What about Jamal?"

"Well," said Peoples, "he's in about the same boat as you, minus the racketeering, money laundering, and such. But rape and attempted rape charges carry a hefty penalty. Trying to flee the country didn't help."

"Give me a chance to think. Work out what you think some decent plea deal scenarios might be for me and Jamal, and get back to me in a couple of days. I've got some serious thinking to do."

"No problem," said Peoples, knowing there were plenty of problems ahead.

Peoples knew that Mayor Brown wanted either no time behind bars for him and Jamal or minimal time in county lockup. He also knew that the prosecution, in no way, was ever going to stipulate to either condition. These were serious big-house crimes and would merit serious big-house time. He wondered if Mayor Brown would come to his senses and realize such. Such was doubtful.

CHAPTER 95

"Do you have a date set yet to start court proceedings against the Browns?"

That question was posed to Prosecutor Luzier by Lt. Riney. It was a Monday morning in late June. Assembled in the prosecutor's office were Lt. Riney, Assistant Prosecutor Stephens, Luzier, and Sheriff Mandela.

"Not as of yet," answered Luzier. "We've got a lot of things to sift through in the meantime."

Luzier's wheels had already been turning. He had gone over all the different scenarios that could play out as a result of the latest events involving the Browns. In his mind, any scenario he had come up with had a favorable outcome for his office.

Luzier informed the group, "I have a meeting set up tomorrow afternoon with Mr. Peoples. He wants to see what kind of plea deals might be on the table for his clients. I'm sure he's not looking for any soft deals."

"He might not be, but I'm sure Mayor Brown is," remarked Lt. Riney. "You can bet on that."

"I've never had much dealings with Mr. Brown. Is he that naive?" asked Sheriff Mandela.

"I wouldn't call it naive," said Assistant Prosecutor Stephens. "He just thinks he's privileged and should be treated as such."

"Gotcha," acknowledged Sheriff Mandela. "Maybe he needs to be shown that privilege doesn't play here."

"You better believe it. Let's send a message," said Luzier.

CHAPTER 96

The Browns were in unfamiliar territory. They were having to deal with uncomfortable circumstances, having to tolerate unsavory characters.

The Browns were in total lockup ever since their capture and arrest five days ago in Anna Maria Island, Florida. They were to have a bond hearing in two days. As explained to them by their attorney, Mr. Peoples, it was unlikely they would be granted any bail due to already having proven themselves to be flight risks.

That lavish home of theirs would have to sit empty for a long time. No longer open for entertaining the local, state, or any other level VIPs. No more entering through the private gates, traveling up the long drive in one of five luxury vehicles to cut themselves off from the underfortunate portion of the world. Not only could they not cut themselves off from the underfortunate population, they were now cohabitating with some of them daily.

Jamal was having the hardest time with it all. He no longer had adoring fans all around. He no longer had his own personal entourage. He was no longer dressed daily in the most expensive, most fashionable outfits. The orange-striped county jumpsuit was not his style.

Jamal was quickly finding out that his father's money, power, and/or influence carried no weight in the Buchanan County Detention Center. He ran across several people in there that he had seen and known on the outside. They recognized him and remembered how he had treated them when they were on the outside. It wasn't very nice. Jamal knew by the looks he was given, he was not well liked. Matter of fact, he felt hated.

The biggest thing for Jamal was coming to the realization that Daddy's magic was gone. Daddy could no longer fix things. Without Daddy there, what was he to do? For the first time he could remember, he felt alone, vulnerable, weak, and scared.

A sheltered, protected, privileged life has its drawbacks.

CHAPTER 97

Mr. Peoples was meeting with Prosecutor Luzier. The two were trying to hash out some kind of deal for both Jamal Brown and his father.

"What are you willing to offer?" asked Peoples.

"Who you want to start with?" was Luzier's question.

"Well, let's start with Jamal."

"With him, I would say that if he is willing to plead guilty to the attempted rape, the sexual assaults, and the fleeing from prosecution, I would say twenty years, with having to serve 85 percent of the sentence, minimum."

"Wow. They're going to think that's a little harsh," stated Peoples.

"What he did was harsh," retorted Luzier. "If he doesn't want to take that, we are willing and ready to go ahead with a trial. They've got to realize that if convicted, he's easily looking at thirty-plus years."

"Any other options?" questioned Peoples.

"That's what I'm willing to offer—twenty years or trial."

"I know the mayor is not going to like those choices," said Peoples. "Speaking of the mayor, what can you offer him?"

"As far as he is concerned," began Luzier, "He's looking at substantial time also. With several more people coming onboard to turn state's evidence, it looks pretty bleak for the mayor. That's just the evidence in the trafficking, money laundering, and evidence tampering."

"What about the fleeing?" inquired Peoples.

"What we found on that boat says a lot about his intentions and is pretty incriminating. Those suitcases had over $40,000 in cash.

Plus the fake passports, wigs, mustaches, and beards. We've got people to say what those were for."

"A tough mountain to climb," said Peoples.

"True," agreed Luzier. "I'm willing to go twenty-five with 85 percent minimum. Just let him know that a conviction at trial, I'm asking for a minimum of forty."

Peoples said, "I understand. I'm assuming that is your only offer."

"It is."

"Well, I will let you know what they say after I deliver the news. I kind of already told the mayor not to expect too much."

"By the way, how are the two doing all locked up?" asked Luzier.

"The mayor's getting by, and Jamal is having a tough time. It's a big change for the two. A big change."

"I know it is. I know it is."

Prosecutor Luzier's job had become consistently repetitive recently. It seemed that every defendant was looking for some sort of plea deal. It didn't seem like any of them wanted a trial because they didn't know who had turned on them and became witnesses for the prosecution. To save themselves any grief, they wanted to make a deal.

Save one's own skin the best way you can. That seemed to be the rule of the day.

Chapter 98

The power couple of Buchanan County had fallen from grace. Their reputation was tarnished. Their influence was diminished. The relationship itself was on shaky ground.

Sgt. Jase Estes was doing a lot of soul-searching. He never thought he would end up in such a predicament. His life and career were on a straight trajectory toward success. Why did it take a change of direction? Why did it take a detour? He tried to deny the reason. But time and time again, it kept revealing itself. As he looked at Jaylyn Reese, as she sat on the couch across the room from him, he could feel the emotions fighting each other within him. Peace versus anger. Love versus hate. It was excruciating.

Jaylyn saw things in a different light. She seemed unfazed by what went down. She did no reflecting, no soul-searching. She looked at how she could continue on her present, at least what she perceived as undisturbed, trajectory. She saw the situation as a mere bump in the road. As she looked at Sgt. Estes, as he sat on the recliner across the room from her, she could feel a warm glow within. She believed he felt the same way.

Such was the thinking of the two members of what, at one time, was the most notable couple of Buchanan County. They seemed, at one time, to be so in love. So attached. So into each other. So entrenched in Buchanan County's elite social circle. So invincible.

Was there now a chink in their armor? Was there now a crack in their protective shield?

It's funny how the charm and perceived persona of one person can reel in the trust and love of another to the point of causing them to go against their normal moral innate values, getting them involved in things that they know could jeopardize their good name and social standing.

The same thing has happened to many of us in some form or fashion. We meet someone and we fall head-over-heels in love. The next thing we know, we are doing things or allowing things to be done that are totally against our nature. We are so enthralled with that person that we don't recognize, or refuse to recognize, what they have gotten us into, how they have managed to change our perception of right and wrong. They get us to believe that the dark side is not so bad, that it too is appealing.

Why does that happen? How does that happen? Can we guard against such a thing happening to us? Can we protect ourselves from that awesome aura of love?

But if you really think about it, what's love got to do with it?

CHAPTER 99

Over the next couple of weeks, a lot of dominoes fell. No one wanted a trial, save one—Mayor Deiondre Brown.

Kenneth Peoples had a constant argument on his hands. The bond hearing went as Peoples had predicted—denied. Ever since, Mayor Brown complained about the unfair treatment he felt he was getting. In order to get back at the justice system, he demanded to go to trial. He wanted the world to see how wrongly he had been charged and locked up, denied his freedom of movement while awaiting trial, denied his rights as an upstanding American citizen.

Peoples constantly informed him of the high-stakes gamble he was going to be taking. He reminded him of the numerous highly credible witnesses the prosecution had lined up to testify against him. He reminded him of how he had attempted to flee the country. He reminded him of his son, who was still counting on him to somehow come to his rescue. He reminded him of the possibility of spending forty-plus years behind bars as opposed to less than twenty-five.

Mayor Brown didn't care. He wanted his day in court. Peoples was dumbfounded. He could not understand why Mayor Brown refused to admit that an acquittal was all but impossible. A trial by jury or bench trial would have the same outcome—guilty—no matter the venue or the judge.

Peoples finally came to the conclusion that Mayor Brown was a desperate man trying to delay the inevitable. Brown's logic and rationale had vanished. In its place were full-blown narcissism, egotism, and self-preservation. Case in point, when asked what he wanted done with his son, Jamal's, predicament, he responded, "I don't care what you do. I've got to take care of my own problems. He can figure it out for himself."

Hmmm. To some, self is all that matters. They'll turn their back on those closest to them in an attempt to save themselves. Where's the loyalty? Where's the unconditional love of family?

Mayor Deiondre Brown must have been absent when those were being handed out.

CHAPTER 100

It'd been several weeks since Lametrius Brewer had contacted Kaneisha. By all signs, it appeared that things were going well. They had seen each other quite a few times for lunch, dinner, or movie dates, and now they were sitting at a restaurant table with their son and new daughter-in-law, Koen and Jolene.

"How's that new house coming along?" asked Brewer.

"It's coming along just fine," answered Jolene.

"Speaking of that, Jolene and I feel a little uneasy about being there and not paying a mortgage or rent. It doesn't seem right," added Koen.

"You're just like your mother," Brewer said. "Not that that's a bad thing." He looked at Kaneisha. "It's a gift, son. A gift. It's all yours. Enjoy it."

"It's just that it's so hard to believe," commented Jolene. "It's such a great place, and we didn't have to do anything to get it."

Kaneisha joined in. "Good things happen to good people, and you two are certainly that. Besides, Koen is doing his father a great service. You can't put a price on that."

"That is so true," Brewer agreed.

It was a lovely evening out. The four truly enjoyed one another's company. Several times through the evening, Kaneisha would sit back and smile and think to herself, *This is what I've always envisioned, what I've always wanted. I hope it's real and forever.*

Brewer asked, "How's the counseling business going?"

"It's great," answered Jolene. "We are superbusy. Next school year, the SMART program is going to expand. Your son's idea was awesome."

"Hold on now," interjected Koen. "It wasn't just me. It was both of us. I couldn't have done it by myself."

"You two are a pretty awesome couple," complimented Kaneisha. "Keep that in mind. You may be good individually, but you're awesome together. Always strive to be awesome."

Is the Brewer family moving toward reconciliation? Only time will tell.

CHAPTER 101

Among the many plea deals Prosecutor Luzier had to make, one was especially gratifying for him. It was the case of Hailey Crawford.

She had been through so much. Her adult life was filled with abuse and manipulation. She was an emotionally and psychologically beaten woman. She had been stabbed to within an inch of her life.

Luzier was impressed with her resiliency, her toughness, her inner fighting spirit. Plus her outright courage came to the surface when she decided to divulge her knowledge of the massive drug-trafficking operation involving many of the notables of the city of Elwood and Buchanan County.

Hailey was a woman who could have cashed it in years ago, a woman that could have succumbed to the pressure and torment from others. Instead, it seemed that an ember of hope and redemption always glowed deep within. Not until the circumstances of the past seven to eight months did the winds of affliction fan that ember, causing it to turn into a flame, a flame of conviction, determination, and righteousness.

These were the things Luzier took into consideration when deciding the charge and penalty for said charge. When it was all said and done, Hailey was charged with aiding and abetting a criminal enterprise and was credited with time served.

The last time Brayden saw his mother, Hailey, was months ago. At the time, he didn't know if she was going to live or die. But now, he was finally going to get to see her, finally going to get to hug her, finally going to get to walk out into the streets with her.

Brayden sat in the prosecutor's office, waiting impatiently for his mother to arrive. Finally around 11:30 a.m., the door opened.

There stood Hailey. At first he didn't recognize her. She no longer looked like the downtrodden woman she once was. She no longer looked like the verbally and physically abused woman of years of torment. She no longer looked like a woman at death's door. She looked healthy, strong, and beautiful. There was a glow about her that Brayden had never seen.

Brayden was ecstatic. He leapt to his feet and ran to his mother's open arms. They embraced for a long time. Both were crying and unable to speak. Words were not necessary. The image of the two said it all.

Prosecutor Luzier, wiping a tear from his eye, eventually said, "Are you two going to stay like that for the rest of the day?"

Hailey, not loosening her hold, replied, "Just maybe. It's been years since I've held my baby this way. It feels so wonderful!"

"Mom, I've missed you so much," Brayden said.

"Oh, I've missed you too, my son. And thank you. Thank you for helping me open my eyes. Thank you for giving me the strength to do what I needed to do."

Brayden replied, "I didn't give you that strength. You had it all along. You had it all the time, Mama."

The two finally broke their embrace. They stared at each other. They couldn't believe this day had come. They were finally free. Free from that prison constructed and maintained by Warden Tyler Davis. No longer did he have control. No longer did he have a say in how they lived their lives. What a feeling!

Luzier said, "I just want to thank the two of you for all that you've done. Without you, we never would have been able to crack such a big operation and take down so many big players. We'll be forever grateful."

"You know," began Hailey, "I'm just so grateful that I was given the opportunity to do the right thing."

Brayden added, "Yeah, Mom, sometimes people are given the chance to do the right thing, but they don't. You did. You made the choice to step up. I'm very proud of you."

"I'm very proud of her too," added Detective Sam Pope, who also was present in the room. "She showed me a lot of courage and determination during the time we spent together. And she did a lot of growing during that time. Growth that will carry her forward. You're a great lady, Hailey Crawford. It's been a joy and a pleasure to get to know you. I consider myself lucky to be able to call you my friend. I hope you consider me to be a friend of yours."

"You better believe I do! You are the best, Sam. You know, as I think about it, I don't think I've actually had a true friend since junior high."

"Well, you've got one now," affirmed Sam.

Hailey said, "I know we probably can't hang out and such, but I sure would like to keep in touch. That would be great."

"You never know about that hanging out thing," replied Sam. "We'll have to check into that. As far as keeping in touch, that for sure will happen."

"Okay, not that I'm trying to get rid of everybody, but I have some other work to do. Besides, I'm sure there are better places you would like to be other than in this office. So take off, be safe, and enjoy. Again, thanks," said Luzier.

CHAPTER 102

"I leave in a couple days for preseason workouts and stuff, and he still hasn't come around," lamented Rey. "He barely says two words at a time to me."

"I'm sorry to hear that. I thought for sure he would have gotten over it by now," commented Bella.

It was mid-July, and Rey was days away from leaving home and starting her college basketball life. She knew it would be a big change and huge adjustment; even more so without her dad's support and encouragement.

Rey's existence began differently than most of us. Her birth mother was a crack addict. Being pregnant did not stop, or even slow down, the usage. Thus Reahlin was born a crack-addicted baby.

Needless to say, the first year and a half to two years were very troublesome. There were many hours of screaming and crying. Screaming and crying because the pains of withdrawal were so excruciating for baby Reahlin.

Fortunately something came across the crack-addicted mother, and she realized she could not take care of herself and a little baby. So she took the baby to an orphanage and left her. Never to see each other again.

When Reahlin was four years old, Coach Mac and his wife Lucille came into the picture. They had tried for years to conceive, but unfortunately, they could not. So they decided to adopt. They had been looking for some time by the time they saw Reahlin. They were immediately drawn in. Reahlin was, in a like manner, drawn to Coach Mac and Lucille. It truly was love at first sight.

They were informed about the issues relating to the crack addiction birth. They didn't care about that. They knew they had found the child they wanted to adopt. Reahlin was the one. In a little more than a year, she was their daughter.

Coach Mac and Lucille were great parents from day one. Did they do everything perfect? Not hardly, but what parent does? But they were always there to talk, teach, discipline, and, most importantly, love and support.

Rey was a happy, energetic, talented, intelligent, independent child. She was a child that adhered to discipline. She learned from her mistakes. She was loving and caring. On top of all that, she was athletically gifted. Not only was she good, but she had an innate desire to always want to get better. That was right up Coach Mac's alley.

As Rey grew and blossomed, so did the dreams for her from Coach Mac and Lucille. They dreamed of a lucrative professional career for her, not just athletically. They dreamed of her finding a prince charming that would treat her like a queen. They dreamed of someday paying for a beautiful church-filled wedding and joyous reception. They dreamed of two or three rambunctious grandchildren running them ragged.

Dreams are just that—dreams. Especially when you have them for others, because they're not obligated to follow your script.

"I don't know if he'll ever get over it," continued Rey. "But you know, I've got to focus on the task at hand, and that's playing ball. That's my meal ticket. It's paying for my college."

Bella nodded. "I wish I could go with you."

"You had your chance. They wanted to offer you a scholarship too."

"I know," Bella acknowledged. "They didn't have the forensics program I was looking for. Other than that, it would've been great being there with you."

"I know. I'll be all right, though. I know some of the girls from prior competitions. They're pretty cool. It'll all be fine."

"For sure. I'm going to really miss you," confessed Bella.

"Shoot. You'll forget me as soon as I walk out that door. You'll be too busy with Brayden."

"Not hardly," argued Bella with a smile. "Ain't never forgetting you. No matter who's in my life."

Two friends getting prepared to venture down separate paths but pledging lasting support and loyalty forever. That's what friends are for.

CHAPTER 103

"What! What do you mean?" asked a shocked Jamal.

Mr. Peoples explained, "Well, he said you are going to have to figure it out yourself. He's got to take care of his own problems."

"What? I don't get it. How does he figure I can do that? What?"

For all his life, Jamal's dad had been there for him, coming to his rescue, making a way out of any kind of predicament. Jamal was clearly upset and bewildered.

"Let me spell it out for you, Jamal. This is what the prosecution is offering as a plea deal."

"I don't want a plea! I'm not saying I did anything!" Jamal was very defiant.

"Jamal, just hear me out. It's very important for you to listen to everything I've got to say, very important."

Jamal sat back in the uncomfortable jail chair. He was still visibly upset, yet he was quiet.

Peoples continued, "So here is where your case stands. On the attempted rape charge, once the jury hears that recording, you're basically done. No jury is going to turn a blind eye to that. On top of that, add the other half dozen sexual assault charges. It all demonstrates a disturbing pattern of behavior. Plus we haven't even mentioned your attempt to skip out of the country. Do you see the picture I'm painting?"

Jamal remained silent; not moving, not responding.

Peoples went on. "Now we could go to trial, but I'll have to be up front with you. It would not be a favorable outcome. I've done hundreds of similar cases, and unfortunately, you're facing an impossible climb. To be found guilty, you're looking at thirty-plus years.

The prosecution is willing to let you plead to twenty years with the option of getting out after 85 percent of the time is served. That would be seventeen years. It's your choice, your decision."

Jamal continued to sit there in silence, drumming his fingers on the table. Finally he asked, "What about basketball?"

"Excuse me?" asked a stunned-looking Peoples.

"What about basketball?" repeated Jamal.

"What do you mean what about basketball?" Peoples was more confused.

"I mean, when will I get to play basketball?"

Peoples then realized that Jamal was not thinking logically. Jamal was refusing to grasp the gravity of the moment.

"Jamal, I'm afraid your days of playing in front of an adoring crowd of fans are over. You'll maybe be able to play some pickup games in the prison yard. That will be the extent of it for many years. Sorry to say."

Jamal sat quietly, leaning back and staring at the bland peeling ceiling. He didn't look at Peoples or utter a word. After two minutes of silence, Peoples prepared to leave.

"Well, Jamal, I know you have a lot to think about. I'll let you do that. I'll get back to you in three days. Maybe then you'll have an answer for me."

Jamal then said, "Why would he do that to me? How could he?"

"Who you talking about?" asked Peoples.

"My dad. Why would he do this to me? Why would he leave me hanging? Doesn't he care what happens to me?"

"I wish I had an answer for you, Jamal."

Never before had he had to make an important decision on his own, let alone a decision that would alter the rest of his life. He felt alone. Never in his wildest dreams would he have thought his father would abandon him in his darkest hour. But such was the case.

CHAPTER 104

Two days later, Kenneth Peoples was in a somewhat complicated discussion with Mayor Deiondre Brown. It didn't have to be complicated, but Mayor Brown made it that way.

"What I'm trying to tell you is that the deck is truly stacked against you. There is no way I can see you winning this," asserted Peoples.

"So you're telling me that you're not capable of rendering me an adequate defense?" questioned Mayor Brown.

"I'm telling you that no one would be able to get the outcome you're looking for. Not even Lametrius Brewer," retorted Peoples.

"To hell with Brewer! I never liked him anyway. Look, it seems to me that you have already decided to sell me down the river. I want a trial! I want somebody that believes they can get me an acquittal!"

"Mr. Mayor," Peoples said, "I can say we are going to trial. All that is going to do is fatten my bank account because no matter how much time I spend, I will not be able to refute the multitude of witnesses the prosecution has testifying against you, the multitude of very credible witnesses. Now you can fire me and find someone else, but I guarantee, you are going to find yourself in the same boat. No one is going to be able to pull off the miracle defense that you want. No one."

"It can be done! I've seen it done!" Mayor Brown argued.

"When?" asked Peoples.

"Well, the O. J. trial. Casey Anthony. Or, or the George Zimmerman trial. See, it can be done!" Mayor Brown continued to argue.

"Those are entirely different cases, different circumstances. Somehow reasonable doubt was established. In your case, not a chance. I've been at this a long time, and I know the prosecution knows they have a slam dunk. I'm asking you to please believe me. I know what I'm talking about."

Mayor Brown responded, "I'm not 100 percent sure I believe you. I may need to find someone else. Someone who has a more open view about things."

"Are you saying you're firing me?"

"No, I'm just saying I've got more thinking to do."

"I see. Okay then. Well, since I have you here for a moment, I wanted to let you know that Jamal is in a pretty bad way."

"What do you mean?" asked Mayor Brown.

"He's feeling abandoned. Left all alone. Is there anything you want me to tell him?"

Mayor Brown thought for a moment, then said, "Tell him to rely on what I've always taught him."

"And that is what?" asked Peoples.

"He'll know," answered Mayor Brown.

Peoples thought to himself that the only thing Jamal had ever been taught was that Daddy would always get him out of any situation. But as it stood, Daddy was too deep in his own circumstances.

Peoples knew that the next time he met with Jamal, it was not going to be encouraging as far as Jamal was concerned.

Chapter 105

"I'm so happy for you! I can only imagine how you felt," said an excited Bella.

Brayden responded, "It was unbelievable! I knew I missed her, but, man! Plus she looked better than I'd ever seen her. She was like a new woman!"

Brayden, two days after seeing his mom for the first time in months, was still beaming and overjoyed. He was reliving the experience with Bella. He was on cloud nine. He now had two wonderful women in his life. As far as he was concerned, it didn't get any better than that.

"I can't wait until she meets you," said Brayden.

"I can't wait to meet her," said Bella. "But what if she doesn't like me?"

Brayden gave Bella a puzzled look and asked, "What are you talking about? Why wouldn't she?"

"Well, sometimes mothers can be pretty picky when it comes to a significant other for their son. That person has to meet certain standards, you know. Besides, she might not want to share you now that you two have been reunited."

"I'm not worried about that. She's going to be wondering how I was able to run across someone like you, let alone date you. I'm quite confident you'll exceed any expectations of any woman she had pictured for me."

"I hope you're right."

"Oh, I am. Believe it."

"By the way," Bella continued, "are you two going to have to testify in any upcoming trials or anything?"

"Well, according to Mr. Luzier, that shouldn't be necessary. He says he has a slew of people, including my dad, that are willing to testify in exchange for leniency in their own cases. Unless they all change their minds or are knocked off, we should be home free. How about you?"

"Basically the same thing. He said he's 98 percent sure Jamal's going to accept a plea deal. He told me not to spend a lot of time thinking about any court stuff. He wants me to concentrate on getting started at college. If I'm needed, it won't be until midsemester, but it's not likely."

Brayden stared off into space for a few seconds, then said, "At one point in time, we were wrapped up in a whole lot of mess happening all around us. Granted, we were worried yet determined to do what was necessary to see that the right thing was done."

"I know," agreed Bella. "At times, it seemed like it was each of us against the world. Sometimes I wondered where I got the inner strength to keep my head up and keep moving forward. Then I thought about all the prayers I prayed. Right then, I knew where that strength came from. God answers prayers and much more."

"Amen," responded Brayden.

Two young people with so much courage and fortitude. Not only that but an unshakeable faith. Would such traits continue to be their foundation as they moved on into adulthood and the real world? Related to these two, it would be a safe bet to say yes, it would.

CHAPTER 106

Several days after his discussions with Mayor Brown, Kenneth Peoples had the unenviable task of talking to Jamal and delivering the so-called words of encouragement from his father.

When Jamal was brought to the visiting room, Peoples gave him a good look over. He saw that Jamal was a beaten young man; a young man that appeared lost. He looked like a young man who didn't have a friend in the world; a young man that had lost all hope.

As Jamal sat down, Peoples felt compelled to ask, "How are you doing?"

"How do you think I'm doing?" Jamal snapped back.

"That was a sincere question, Jamal. I worry about you. I want to make sure you're okay, and if I can do anything for you to make things better, just let me know, and I'll see what I can do."

"How about getting me out of here? That would make everything a lot better."

"I'm afraid that can't happen. Everybody treating you all right?"

Jamal shrugged and said, "I guess, all things considering. There are a couple guys who are being jerks, but no big deal."

"They haven't gotten physical, have they?" asked Peoples.

"Nah. They just like runnin' off at the mouth. Hey, did you talk to my dad? What did he have to say?"

Peoples didn't really want to answer that question, but he knew he had to.

"Yes, I did talk to him."

Peoples hesitated for a second. Jamal jumped in. "What did he say?"

"He said to tell you to rely on what he's always taught you."

Jamal squinted and said, "What the hell does that mean? Is that all he said?"

"That is all he said. Evidently he feels he has taught you some very important decision-making lessons. He suggested you use those lessons in figuring out what you want to do with your situation."

Jamal grew furious. He said nothing, but it was obvious by the scowl on his face and the clenching of his fists. Peoples let him stew for a couple minutes.

"This might not be the best time, but I have to ask. Have you decided what you want to do? Plea or what?"

Jamal continued to sit in silence. By watching his eyes, it was easy to see what emotions he was experiencing. There was anger. Then hate. Then hurt. Back to anger. Back and forth. For minutes.

Finally Peoples said, "Jamal, I need an answer."

Jamal sat up in his chair. He looked down at the floor, then up at the ceiling. With his head leaning back, and a tear streaming out of his left eye, he reluctantly said, "I'm going to plead."

"Are you sure?" Peoples asked.

Jamal nodded.

"So you're telling me you're going to plea to attempted rape and five counts of sexual assault and sexual harassment for a sentence of twenty years with a minimum of 85 percent served? Is that correct?"

Jamal nodded and quietly said, "Yes."

"All right. I will take this to the prosecutor and let them know your decision. When he sets a court date, I will let you know. Now, Jamal, it might not seem like it right now, but that was probably a smart choice. It is a long time, but it could have been worse. Believe me, it could have been worse."

Jamal stared blankly ahead. Peoples wondered what he was thinking.

Jamal then asked, "Are you going to see my dad any time soon?"

"I will see him in a couple days. Is there a message you want to send him?"

"Yeah, there is," said Jamal. "Tell him I hope he rots in hell!"

Jamal got up and was escorted out by the guard.

CHAPTER 107

"As it looks, Tyler," began Prosecutor Luzier, "Mayor Brown is the only one that seems hard-pressed on going to trial. But that was as of last week. He could have changed his mind. I'll meet with his attorney tomorrow, so I'll know more at that time."

"Why does he have to do this?" asked Tyler. "I don't understand it."

"Some people refuse to give in. The mayor is one of those people," answered Luzier.

"He worries me," said Tyler. "He could still have people take me out. Make his life easier."

"I'm pretty sure his sphere of influence has shrunk quite a bit here lately. He doesn't carry the weight he used to," assured Luzier.

That didn't seem to ease the mind of Tyler Davis. He was a natural worrier. He could be locked in a concrete bunker on the remotest of islands, with an armed military unit guarding the only entrance, and he would still feel unsafe. His paranoia always seemed to get the best of him.

One thing he had not lost a feel for was his feelings for Hailey. He constantly wondered how she was doing. He wanted to know she was safe and taken care of. He missed her. He loved her. But he did not know how she felt about him.

"Can I ask you something?" Tyler inquired of Luzier.

"Sure. Go ahead."

"How is Hailey?"

"She is doing just fine," Luzier said.

"That's good to hear," commented Tyler. "I worry about her, you know. Do you think it would be possible for me to see her for a minute or two?"

"As things stand right now, that would not be possible. Too much is still going on."

Tyler wanted to know. "Does she ever ask about me?"

"Actually, I haven't heard her ask about you, but that's not to say she hasn't asked someone else, just not me."

Tyler was disappointed yet not surprised. He had had plenty of time to think about the life he and Hailey had spent together. He knew it had not always been the best of times. He knew he had not been the most pleasant person to be around most of the time. He realized he had put all his time and efforts in keeping his "friends" of illegal activities pleased. With his family, he had been overbearing, unaffectionate, verbally and physically abusive. His family had rated very low on his list of importance.

He realized how wrong he had been. He wished he could take it all back. He wanted a do-over. He wanted Hailey to give him another chance. He was convinced he had changed, and he wanted her to see and experience that change. He just wanted a chance to talk to her, to plead his case.

Not once did he ask about or allow his mind to think about his son, Brayden.

What was that all about?

CHAPTER 108

"We want to hear what you have to say," said Prosecutor Luzier to Sgt. Jase Estes.

PA Luzier was meeting with Sgt. Estes and Lt. Marcus Riney.

"Well, are you guys still trying to piece together the Browns' attempted escape from prosecution?" asked Sgt. Estes.

"We are," said Luzier.

"Jaylyn arranged it all. She set it all up," confessed Estes.

Lt. Riney was somewhat surprised. "Oh, really. How?"

Sgt. Estes continued, "The mayor had unfailing trust in Jaylyn. There was nothing he didn't let her in on, and there was nothing she wouldn't do to help him out. One did nothing without the other knowing about it. It was unreal.

"Once Mayor Brown figured the phone recording was going to be presented to the jury against Jamal, everything was started. Brown fired Brewer, knowing that would give him more time to think of a plan B. So he got with Jaylyn and began planning to go on the run. I didn't sit in on their meetings, but Jaylyn would always come to me afterward and tell me what was said and what was planned. I guess she felt I was 100 percent in with her and him."

"Well, you were, weren't you?" questioned Luzier.

"I guess I was," lamented Sgt. Estes. "I didn't try to stop her nor did I report what was going on. Hmm, I guess I was."

Luzier and Lt. Riney could tell that Sgt. Estes was in anguish. He knew he had been manipulated and used. He had allowed that to happen. Once he had let his guard down, it was all over. She had him, and he couldn't break free. Nor did he want to. Lt. Riney could especially see the torment that his former mentor and good friend was going through.

"Man, I just don't know." Sgt. Estes began questioning himself. "How could I have done such? I had so much going for me. I was on that straight and narrow. It was like I couldn't stop what was happening. Like I didn't want to stop it. She was so alluring. It was like Adam and Eve. She put that temptation in front of me, and I chose not to ignore it. I just grabbed it up and ran with it. What was I thinking? I'll never figure it out."

Lt. Riney commented, "Don't keep beating yourself up, man. Ease that burden by telling Luzier all you know about what Jaylyn did. Okay?"

Sgt. Estes shook his head and continued, "I've got plenty of time for a self-beatdown. Now where was I?" A short pause. "Oh, yeah. Now I'm probably sure you looked into Brown's finances. Looked at the big withdrawals made just prior to his departure."

"We have," said Luzier.

"Well, the closer you look into those and follow that money, you'll see those were all for legitimate transactions. Those monies were used to pay off legit debts. They can all be verified. Brown didn't want any lingering debts once he was gone. That would put extra people wanting to find him. He didn't want that at all."

"What about the suitcases full of cash, about forty grand? What's up with that?" Luzier asked.

"That money all came from Jaylyn. She put all that together," answered Sgt. Estes.

Luzier was shocked. "How did she come up with all that money?"

"That's only a drop in the bucket," asserted Sgt. Estes. "She has plenty more where that came from. You're going to need to apply for a couple of search warrants and put some surveillance on Jaylyn because she is getting nervous and wanting to move some assets. She has millions—that's right—millions stashed away in a couple of safes at a couple of properties."

Lt. Riney and Luzier had stunned looks upon their faces.

Sgt. Estes continued, "As of right now, I've convinced her to lay low for a minute. I told her too much activity on her part might draw too much attention. But I don't know how long she'll be willing to lay low. She's really anxious to start moving things."

"You got all the information needed for the search warrants?" asked Luzier.

"I do," answered Sgt. Estes.

"What about Jaylyn?" asked Lt. Riney. "Where's she right now?"

"She's waiting on me to get back. I told her I was meeting you to discuss putting off any hearings until months down the road. She still thinks she has me 100 percent under control."

"Does she?" asked Lt. Riney.

"No. Not anymore," answered Sgt. Estes. "I know I screwed up big-time. I've told myself that I've got to atone for my mistakes. They'll never be erased, but I know I can still do some good."

"Let's get to work," suggested Luzier.

Adam and Eve. Superman's kryptonite. Both are so fitting. A fall from grace. A loss of power.

CHAPTER 109

The next ten months were very interesting for all the major players in the past year's dramas in Elwood and Buchanan County, for different reasons, of course.

Koen and Jolene saw their counseling service establish a solid foundation and reputation. The number of clients increased dramatically.

That increase did not include the expansion of the SMART program. Through the first semester of the new school year, the numbers went from ten students to twenty-nine. That, while it's great for their business, was a commentary on the attitudes and behaviors of the students of the high schools the program serviced.

Koen and Jolene simply knew they had a job to do and welcomed the extra workload. They believed in their ability to help and make a change. Their clientele believed in them also.

Another addition was on its way as well. Two days before Halloween, the young couple found out they were going to be parents. Needless to say, they were ecstatic. The Brewer legacy would continue on.

Speaking of the Brewer legacy, the architect of that legacy was, of course, Lametrius Brewer. He definitely had put the name on the map.

But now, a new chapter had begun for him. He officially retired. A once-lucrative practice closed its doors. Arguably, the best defense attorney in the region was not going to be making any more arguments. Those accused of various offenses would no longer be able to enlist his services. They were bumming. Brewer was not.

He was loving retirement. He realized how good free time was. He could do what he wanted, when he wanted, where he wanted.

He had amassed a small fortune. He had all the toys he needed and didn't need. Retirement helped him realize one other thing—how much he loved Kaneisha.

Now that he no longer needed to establish himself as the best at his craft, no longer needing to chase down the finer material things in life, he saw that something was missing. That something was his family. He was missing the thrill, the excitement, the emotional roller coaster of family life. More importantly, he was missing the love of a family, the love he had once shared with Kaneisha, with Kaneisha and Koen.

When they divorced, neither Lametrius nor Kaneisha ever got serious with anyone else. She was in love with Lametrius. Lametrius himself was too self-absorbed to devote any time to a serious relationship. Kaneisha was greatly hurt by the divorce, but something inside her kept believing that the real Lametrius Brewer would emerge, and she wanted to be around if and when it happened. It appeared Kaneisha's patience and belief paid off.

The two were slowly, steadily, moving back into a serious loving relationship. Both were overjoyed with having rediscovered each other. The future looked bright for the couple.

*****

Hailey Crawford became a new woman. She was confident, radiant, and energetic. She found a full-time job at an animal shelter. She had always wanted a pet, but Tyler wouldn't allow it. Now in essence, she had plenty. She absolutely loved it.

As if working forty hours a week weren't enough, she volunteered up to twenty hours a week at a homeless shelter. Her work and volunteering were truly gratifying. She felt alive again. She felt useful and productive. She felt reborn.

Right before Thanksgiving, Hailey had decided to visit Tyler in the Buchanan County Detention Center. She had heard he wanted to see her. She wanted to talk to him too.

What she saw was a frail, unkempt, disheveled shell of a man. What she saw deeply saddened her.

They sat and talked for about an hour. Tyler repeatedly talked about how sorry he was for the way he had treated her. He professed to be a changed man. He wanted her to consider giving him another chance. He expressed his love for her and how much he missed her. Hailey was not swayed.

She knew if he was a changed man, he would have asked about Brayden. Not once did he mention their son. That told Hailey that Tyler did not want Brayden around, and if he could not accept and love their son, he would have no place in Hailey's life. When she left the detention center, she vowed never to see Tyler Davis again.

Brayden Davis was doing just fine. The love of his life, Isabella Seger, had gone to college, and he was in Elwood working at the local Home Depot. It was full-time work. He made decent money, and it kept him out of trouble. He had told his mother and Bella that he wasn't going to get content and stay at Home Depot for years. He wanted to go to college. He just hadn't figured out where or what to major in. Another thing that was constantly on his mind was his mother.

He was so grateful that they were finally able to spend quality mother-son time together. When possible, they would go out to eat, see a movie, or even go shopping. They just loved being around each other, not having to worry about the heavy-handed tyranny of Tyler Davis.

Brayden was aware that his father never asked about him, never seemed to care how he was doing. He was okay with that. Because of the deep psychological scars and bruises caused by his father, he didn't care if they ever spoke to each other again.

Brayden had turned eighteen. He knew he was just crossing that threshold of adulthood. He knew that whatever was in the past was just that, in the past. He had to forge on and create his own future. It was all up to him as to how his adult life would pan out. One thing for sure, he was determined to see that it would turn out to be stellar.

*****

Mayor Deiondre Brown was still up to his usual antics. He was still demanding a trial. He actually fired Mr. Peoples two days after the Labor Day holiday. Peoples just wasn't telling him what he wanted to hear. If the truth be told, Peoples was relieved. Mayor Brown went through three more attorneys before deciding on one. He managed to get his trial date pushed back to the end of February. Still, that seemed too soon to the mayor.

One peculiar thing began to surface, the behavior of the mayor. It was strange and erratic. He was observed constantly mumbling and talking to himself. He paced incessantly. His nails were bitten to the quick. He rarely shaved or showered. He seemed to be getting more and more forgetful. He was easily agitated. He even got into several scuffles at the detention center. All these things were uncharacteristic for Mayor Brown. The mayor had always given the appearance of being in control and under control. What was going on with him? What was happening to his mind?

Some observers were not buying into the belief that Mayor Deiondre Brown was having a mental breakdown. To them, it was another masterful performance of manipulation and deceit perpetrated by the king of fraud. They looked at it as a way for him to stave off actual prison. They felt he was trying to work his way to a commitment to a mental health facility.

One thing that even the detractors had to admit was that what had happened to Jamal would push most parents over the edge.

*****

The elite couple of Elwood and Buchanan County was no more. The fallout was total and complete.

As it turned out, Jaylyn Reese was a much bigger player in the whole scheme of things than anyone had realized. She was an equal partner with the mayor, not a minion.

She took care of the money and saw to it that any books that needed to be cooked were. Any cash that needed to be stashed, she took care of that. And she stashed a lot of cash. A whole lot.

Search warrants were executed on the two residences Sgt. Estes had informed Prosecutor Luzier about. What they found was mind-boggling.

At each of the residences were four very large heavily armed men. SWAT teams were the ones who gained entry to the residences and were able to quickly and quietly neutralize the occupants and secure the premises.

In the one residence, located in a quiet middle-class neighborhood, officers uncovered a cache of weapons, a cache of drugs, and a walk-in safe fitted inside a closet. Inside the safe were stacks and stacks of money—tens, twenties, fifties, hundreds—all neatly bundled and separated. It was incredible to see. In the second residence, located in an upscale neighborhood, officers found the same type of caches and a similar safe setup.

It was clear that by the amount of drugs seized, the criminal drug enterprise never really shut down.

The amount of cash found in the safes totaled $1.6 million. Unbelievable. It was another indication the drug enterprise was still ongoing.

Simultaneous to the raids, Jaylyn Reese was arrested, and a search warrant was executed on the residence she shared with Sgt. Estes. Of major importance were the electronic devices and financial records. Some manual ledgers were also procured.

Sgt. Estes was present when Jaylyn was taken into custody. Because Sgt. Estes showed no surprise and was not taken into custody, Jaylyn immediately knew what had happened. She knew that this was all due to him turning on her. She was surprised yet more so, heartbroken. She felt betrayed.

As she was being led away, she looked at Sgt. Estes. Their eyes met. Through tears, Jaylyn could surmise that there was little empathy in the eyes of Sgt. Estes. It was like he was simply saying she was getting what she deserved, and he didn't feel bad about it. That crushed her. She knew they were done. She had lost a good man and had ruined that good man's reputation.

Sgt. Estes was feeling no empathy. As a matter of fact, he was feeling a small sense of vindication. He had, in effect, taken down the drug queen of Buchanan County. But not before he himself had been taken down. He felt sorry for Jaylyn but sorrier for himself.

He knew he had been seduced by a modern-day temptress. He had no one to blame but himself. He had thrown away an excellent successful career. What hurt the most was the ruining of a stellar reputation. He was revered, a role model, an example of class and style. That was all wiped away. He was going to have to try to rebuild his reputation, his character, his trustworthiness. His climb to the top was swift. His fall was much faster and very painful.

As a result of his cooperation with the prosecution, Sgt. Estes was offered a plea deal. He accepted. He pled guilty to tampering with evidence and aiding a criminal enterprise. He was given a sentence of thirty-seven months, SIS (suspended imposition of sentence). Some probably thought he got off easy, but in reality, his actual punishment was much worse than any jail time.

*****

At the end of August, Jamal Brown pled guilty to the attempted rape and several counts of sexual assault and harassment. As agreed upon, he received a twenty-year sentence with minimum of 85 percent of the term mandatory.

At the proceeding, Jamal appeared to be in a good mental state. He was alert, upbeat, and unusually positive about the whole thing. Mr. Peoples was surprised at Jamal's demeanor but relieved to see him in such a good mood. But as it turned out, such a drastic change in attitude was actually a red flag for what was to come.

The judge announced the sentence and remanded custody over to the Buchanan County Sheriff's Department. Jamal was escorted out of the courtroom by two deputies for his return to the detention center.

Brayden and Aunt Alicia were present in the courtroom. They were there to represent Bella who was away at college. After hearing the plea and subsequent sentence, they both felt a sense of relief and closure. They felt that everyone could finally start to put all of this in the rearview mirror, especially Bella.

They did take notice that even though Jamal had an upbeat attitude, physically he looked weak. He had always been in great shape and very muscularly toned. He had lost that. Having spent several months in jail, there was no more tone, no more Adonis-like facade. He actually looked frail. They surmised that he just hadn't had a chance for regular exercise or a healthy meal choice. However, it was something much deeper.

Ever since the plea, Jamal's mental state rapidly declined. He became deeply depressed. His father was not able to fix things for him. As a matter of fact, his dad didn't even have a desire to help him. His dad had abandoned him. Jamal felt alone, helpless, and betrayed. He no longer had his entourage. No more adoring fans. No longer was he the king of the hill. No longer was he able to go as he pleased. No more fancy meals. No more expensive clothes and cars. No more comfortable bed. No more video games. Life as he knew it was gone. Never to be again.

On the morning of his scheduled transfer from the detention center to the medium-security prison in Olathe, Kansas, Jamal, who had been sleeping overnight in a holdover cell, was unresponsive when the guards called out to him. When they opened the cell door, there was Jamal, hanging from the end of the bed by his orange-striped jumpsuit. The guards immediately rushed to him. There was a faint pulse. Medical personnel were notified, and they responded swiftly. Jamal was rushed to the local hospital. It didn't look good. Not good at all.

After about three and a half hours, a surgeon came into the emergency waiting room, looking for the family of Jamal Brown. Present was Camille Brown, his mother. The surgeon informed her that they were able to save Jamal's life. Camille was relieved.

However, the doctor said there was severe damage to the spinal cord at the base of the skull. It appeared, in all likelihood, that he would be paralyzed from the neck down. The news was devastating.

The once-strong athletically gifted individual was now a quadriplegic. The once-promising future was lost. Jamal was, once again, a total dependent. He was going to need someone to move him, to bathe him, to feed him, someone to clothe him. He was back to square one. Was he going to be able to survive such an existence? Was his mental makeup strong enough to push him to survive? It was a question no one could answer.

Camille struggled with the news. Never in her wildest dreams did she envision something like this happening to her son. She was well aware that his father, Mayor Deiondre Brown, had not always been the best teacher of life lessons. He never allowed his son to learn from life. He always took care of everything for Jamal. Jamal never learned to fend for himself or solve his own problems. How was he going to handle this situation, this predicament?

As the months passed, Jamal's condition continued to degrade. Camille did what she could to get his spirit to fight, to not give up. But Jamal was done.

As was evident by his suicide attempt, he didn't want to be around any longer. He had given up on life. His star had been dimmed. He had no desire to be ordinary or less. The one person he had always counted on turned their back on him. They stopped caring about him. Jamal had even begun to wonder if they ever really did care about him, or was it all just to enhance their own image. He felt his best option was to simply end it all. He tried but was not successful. Yet his mind continued toward that desire. He did not want to fight. He did not want to survive.

On Thanksgiving Day, he passed away. A medical reason would be given for his death, but it was simply no desire to live. His mind shut his body down. Camille was crushed. It would take her months just to be able to get back to her normal day-to-day life. Still, it was not the same. Something was missing and always would be.

A tragic loss. A young life ended. Why?

Sometimes a fall from the top of the mountain can have deadly consequences.

*****

Reahlin McCullough, Rey, had packed up in mid-July and had taken her talents to Floyd State University in Atlanta, Georgia. She was there to begin her college basketball career.

Being a freshman, of course, she was subject to some harassment from the older players. It was all in good fun. She actually enjoyed it. She even returned the favor from time to time. The older players loved it. It didn't take them long to fall in love with Rey.

The preseason workouts were grueling. But they did not bother Rey. She was used to such, being the daughter of Coach Mac. Plus she loved being pushed and challenged. That was just who she was, who she had always been. She was not going to change who she was. She had been taught by Coach Mac and Lucille that no matter who tries to get you to change, no matter who turns their back on you, no matter who will not accept you for who you are or what you stand for, don't change who you are. That was what they taught her.

It was extremely painful to reflect on that at that point in time because the one who could not accept her for who she was and what she stood for was her own father. The one who had preached that very principle. The one that meant the world to her. It took a chunk out of her sentimental heart, but at the same time, it added an impetus to her competitive heart. Even if he wouldn't accept her, she was not going to throw away his teachings and words of wisdom.

When regular practices started, Rey quickly established herself as the real deal. The upperclassmen readily conceded that she was the best on the team. But they liked the fact that she was a team player. She did what she had to do when necessary, but she got everyone else involved.

Early on, Rey sat down with one of the senior leaders of the team. She was extremely nervous. She mustered up enough courage to come out to her. She didn't know what to expect. What she found out was, she was not alone. The senior leader told her there were others and that it was not a problem with the rest of the team. An individual's sexual orientation was that person's own business. What was important was the character of the person and, of course, how well they played basketball. Rey was relieved and thrilled. She knew then she could really relax. And relax she did.

When season play began, Rey was sensational. She never slowed down all season. She was arguably the best player in the country.

Floyd State University Lady Dragons were already an up-and-coming basketball program prior to the season. Now they had officially established themselves as a powerhouse. They were a big ticket draw. It was fundamental basketball at its best.

They rolled through the regular season, 24–2. They won their conference post-season tournament. They got an automatic bid in the NCAA tournament and were seeded number 1 in the Midwest Region. They won that region. They made it to the final four and, subsequently, to the championship game.

Floyd State University was the overwhelming favorite. Their opponent was the South Carolina Gamecocks, the Cinderella team of the tourney. Being a regional ninth seed, the Gamecocks had fought and scrapped their way to the championship game. They continued to fight and scrap throughout the championship game. So much so that they scrapped out an unbelievable victory, much to the chagrin of the Lady Dragons. Rey and her teammates were devastated. They were so close. It just wasn't meant to be.

As the Lady Dragons were coming off the floor after watching the South Carolina celebration and heading to the locker room, Rey just happened to glance up into the stands as the team entered the tunnel. There stood Coach Mac and Lucille. They were beaming, clapping, and throwing kisses to Rey. She stopped, ran back, jumped into the stands, and ran to her parents. They hugged for a long time. They hugged. They cried. They kissed. They loved. It was great to see. To Rey, that was better than any championship could have ever been; seeing her parents there, being there to support her, being there to love her. Nothing was better.

True love may, at times, veer off track, but it has a way of righting itself.

*****

Once again, within a year's time, Bella was starting out as a complete stranger in an educational setting. This time, it was college. This was a different feeling, though. This was something she had looked forward to, something she was excited about.

She knew there would be challenges; some the same as high school and many totally different. She just remembered how her mom and dad had always preached to her about being real and true, about keeping priorities straight, no matter the obstacles or distractions that may present themselves.

Bella knew her number 1 priority was education, and she planned accordingly. Fortunately her roommate was just as centered and prioritized. Both enjoyed studying. Neither was a partier. They both liked attending a variety of activities on campus. Studying, however, was first and foremost. They were able to work together if possible and give the other one the room or time to do what they might need to finish an assignment or project. Bella hit the jackpot as far as roommates went.

Bella's hard work paid off the first semester. She made the dean's list, and it looked like the second semester would be no different.

She kept in touch with Rey. They talked a couple times a week and used social media to reach out to each other. She definitely kept up with how Rey's basketball season was going. She wished she was still playing with her. Nevertheless, she was extremely happy for Rey and superproud of her. She bragged about being her friend as often as she could. People were genuinely impressed. She didn't brag to help her own social status; she bragged about how great a person Rey was. She wanted people to know the real Rey.

It just so happened that Rey's Lady Dragons played against South Carolina in the championship game. Bella's roommate's mother was an alum of South Carolina. So the two had their own little watch party. Bella was heartbroken when Floyd State lost. She was, however, overjoyed when she talked to Rey, and Rey told her that Coach Mac and Lucille were at the game. Bella shed tears of joy. So did Rey.

The start of Bella's school year began on somewhat of a sad note. She was saddened by the events surrounding Jamal.

She was relieved that she would not have to get back on the witness stand due to Jamal accepting a plea agreement. But she immediately wondered how that would affect him. She knew that things had changed so drastically and so fast for him. She worried that that might be too much for him to handle. Lo and behold, she was right.

When she got the news about the suicide attempt and the subsequent paralysis, she actually shed a tear. She shed a tear because a young life with so much potential had been led astray. A young life had been falsely led to believe they were invincible. That no matter what they did, it was okay. No matter who they hurt, it was okay. They were led to believe that privilege trumps everything.

Sometimes you can't blame the student. Sometimes it is the teacher that makes the mistake, that disseminates the wrong information. Jamal was the victim of fallible teachings.

Bella felt that Jamal could be a gentleman if he wanted to. But as she thought deeper about that, she figured that maybe that was just a part of his grooming process. *What a shame*, she thought. What a shame.

His death was not a shock to her either. She kind of expected it. She was at home with Aunt Alicia for Thanksgiving break when they got the news. They simply said a prayer of forgiveness for his soul.

While she was home for the holiday break, it gave her a chance to spend some quality time with Brayden. They both enjoyed that immensely.

Their relationship was solid, and it was getting stronger. The strength seemed to grow from their shared experience of having to overcome hardship, though different in nature. They both possessed an inner strength that is uncommon in many people their age. A maturity beyond their years. To look at them, it was plain to see, their love was real, deep, and lasting.

Bella, as a direct influence of her mom and dad, Earl and Donna Seger, was a young woman of high moral character. She wasn't influenced by peer pressure. If she didn't like the way something looked, felt, or sounded, she didn't hesitate to say no and stick to her values. Her mantra was "dedication to right and truth." She lived her life true to her mantra.

*****

Life went on in Elwood and Buchanan County. There were many good times and some not-so-good times. The people tried their best to move on from the ugly recent events, but social media and media outlets would not let them make that move seamlessly. Something was always being posted or relived to remind the citizens of the tragic indiscretions of the past. Guess that's just how life works in this day and age. Others simply won't let you forget.

There were many changes to the power structure of local leadership. Younger adults got more involved in political activities. They brought with them new ideas and broader perspectives. The new faces were a breath of fresh air.

Looking from the outside, it all appeared to be for the better. But as the saying goes, "Looks can be deceiving."

EPILOGUE

We are all influenced by our surroundings. To what degree is varying. A lot depends on who and/or what we encounter and what direction we are taken by those encounters.

In societies, no matter how civilized or uncivilized, generations teach successive generations. Cultural and social norms are taught and handed down. Our development, most assuredly, is shaped by what we are taught and what we observe.

In a civilized society, such as the good old USA, there are certain expectations of the one doing the teaching and the one being taught. If you take and examine what is perceived to be a well-rounded individual, certain qualities are possessed. Those particular qualities are to be instilled by the teacher. Note that teacher is not exclusively referring to the classroom variety. The teacher may vary, but the subject matter is the same. The teacher is expected to teach us, what I call, a foundation of human decency, encompassing qualities such as:

- Honor our mother and father
- Show love
- Accept love
- Be grateful
- Be appreciative
- Be open-minded
- Respect others
- Cooperate with others
- Have manners
- Share
- Listen
- Be empathetic

- Be modest
- Show humility
- Be truthful and honest
- Be charitable
- Be resilient
- Have patience
- Be tolerant
- Be accepting
- Be compassionate

This is not an all-encompassing list, but it is a list that helps establish the bricks, or blocks, needed for a good solid foundation of human decency.

But what if something on that list is omitted or forgotten? What effect does that have on an individual's development?

Have you ever known someone that was never taught to share with others? How about someone that doesn't know how to express compassion or empathy? Or one who was never taught humility, truth, and honesty? Have you ever had to work with someone who has no concept of what cooperation is? Have you been around someone who does not appreciate anything or anyone? Or someone who is ungrateful for their many blessings? Or someone who has no tolerance or acceptance for anyone or anything that is different from their own ideas or ideology? What about someone who has no modesty? Have you ever known anyone who did not know how to love or show love or even accept love? Were you ever around someone who refused to respect or honor their parents?

If so, how were those interactions? Were they awkward, trying, frustrating, infuriating, or worse?

Just missing or misusing one of those supposedly taught qualities can have a negative impact on the development of an individual and their subsequent interactions with others.

We are who we are based largely on what we are taught and observe, subsequently, what we allow ourselves to embrace and take hold of and absorb. We are shaped by what those closest to us disseminate and model. If they model love, compassion, respect, acceptance, and humility, we are likely to emulate the same. If they model arrogance, intolerance, nonacceptance, bias, or prejudice, we are likely to project the same.

It is not only our close family that effects our development, it's also our peers, our educators, our neighbors, our extended family members, our occupation, our coworkers, our bosses, our environment. There are innumerable factors that go into making us who we are. All of us have these factors and more. How solid our foundation of human decency is determines how much these factors impact us.

So ask yourself, "How solid is my foundation of human decency? Do I have all the bricks in place, or am I missing one, two, or more?"

At the same time, take a look at your interactions with other people. Are you open-minded or close-minded? Do you accept or just tolerate others that are different from you and/or your views? Are you humble, respectful, grateful, and appreciative? Do others matter less than you? Where is your heart centered? Is it in gold and glory or God and humanity?

How solid is your foundation of human decency? Are all the bricks in place?

Just because a brick or more may be missing does not mean the foundation is irreparable. It does not mean the foundation has crumbled completely. The missing brick, or bricks, can be found and put in the correct spot in the foundation. Just find it and put it in place. The other bricks welcome the added support, the filling of that empty hole. So will you.

We all, at some time or another, have a missing brick or two. To rectify the problem, we have to first recognize we have a missing brick. Also we have to realize that sometimes, we need help. We have to be willing to ask others to help us find that missing piece. There are many willing and able to lend a helping hand. Don't be too prideful or afraid to ask. Failure to act over time will result in a collapse of the foundation.

A crumbling or incomplete foundation can't safely support a priceless piece of art. So the potter gives it the unimportant task of holding the pieces of imperfection, the flawed pieces of clay.

However, a solid foundation proudly supports and exhibits a beautiful artistic piece of art; a piece of perfection, a sensationally molded and crafted piece of clay.

Alvin was born and raised in small-town Missouri, i.e., Crystal City, located about thirty miles south of St. Louis. He was fortunate to grow up in a large, warm, and cohesive family.

Alvin attended Rockhurst College (now Rockhurst University) in Kansas City, Missouri. He did not complete his degree ambition at that time due to starting a family early. As a result, he has three outstanding sons and ten outstanding grandchildren.

He spent thirteen years in law enforcement and then went into a career in education. He and his wife are retired special-education teachers, but Alvin continues to coach high school girls' basketball.

Alvin's two favorite hobbies are writing and coaching.

CPSIA information can be obtained
at www.ICGtesting.com
Printed in the USA
LVHW091258301121
704855LV00005B/76